Saddled for Vengeance

Link Hardmun has done some foul things in his life, but this time he is about to be hanged for a murder he didn't commit – unless the sadistic sheriff beats him to death first. He regrets nothing except missing his chance to catch the real killer, the mad dog Amos Turk. Hobbled and jeered at, Hardmun makes his way up the gallows steps under the watchful eyes of the man who captured him – the nameless old gentleman he's taken to calling the Colonel – and the hate-filled sister of the woman Turk murdered.

But before he can take his last deadly step, Turk and his gang ride in for the rescue, stealing Hardmun for their own brand of vicious justice. Labelled a traitor, Hardmun is marked for death at Turk's own hand. But he escapes and so begins a deadly cat-and-mouse game in the sweltering, cracked lava desert. Can Hardmun live long enough to finally bring the real killer to justice?

By the same author

Valley of Hate

Saddled for Vengeance

Clay Burnham

A Black Horse Western

ROBERT HALE · LONDON

First published in Great Britain 2004

ISBN 0 7090 7532 4

Robert Hale Limited
Clerkenwell House
Clerkenwell Green
London EC1R 0HT

Typeset by
Derek Doyle & Associates, Liverpool.
Printed and bound in Great Britain by
Antony Rowe Limited, Wiltshire

CHAPTER ONE

HANGMAN'S HOLIDAY

An icy sliver of air cut through the desert town of Arango, curling past the false-fronts, kicking up a tiny dust devil.

Morning had not yet broken, the sun only a blood red hint in the eastern sky. Soon it would come, angry and hot, a malevolent force to be endured but never conquered.

People had yet to stir from their beds. Cool sleep was something to be savored in Arango behind the weather beaten false-fronted buildings and in the tiny houses that sat lopsidedly on the cracked desert earth. Blissful peace enveloped the morning with no hint of what was to come. There was excitement to be had this day. Bread and circuses had been a name given it by the ancients; though blood-lust was a name that came easier to the tongues of more modern men.

The good people of Arango would leave their cool beds and the brief respite of night to brave the blistering sun that would soon rise. Blood sport was to be had and few would miss it. They would come into the center of town and stare with mad eyes, half afraid and half grateful not to be the object of attention.

The sun rose, a piercing arrow of light shooting over the far gray hills. The yellow beam cut into town, slicing a sharp path to the top of the newest structure in Arango. It was made of wood, this creation, and smelled still of fresh-cut cedar. A simple frame, really, with a crossbeam and a flimsy railing and thirteen solid steps.

And a spring-loaded trap.

There was a man atop this construct, the only living thing about so early. He smiled beneath his black hood, smiled as he fingered the lever beside the spring-loaded trap. Savagely, he pulled at the lever and the trap door fell open into space with a vicious thud.

The sound echoed through Arango, followed by the cold cruelty of the man's laughter.

Rough hemp tore at the throat of Link Hardmun. Strong arms pinioned his own, vice-like, unrelenting.

He fought to keep calm. The noose placed over his neck had a long tail, and though he knew it was tied to nothing, he couldn't help but hate the thing. Still, deep down he knew he would not hang . . . not yet, not today.

Sheriff Capstin pulled the noose tight, pinching the skin of Hardmun's raw neck. He laughed, that sweating, fat-bellied mule. Laughed because death was thick in the air and the sport of blood was soon to be had.

Capstin rested the neck of the noose on Hardmun's shoulder. The thirteen knots had been made with great care by the lawman. He wouldn't let the hangman make the noose, preferring that pleasure for himself. The knots weighed heavily on Hardmun's shoulder, much heavier than the sheriff or his two cackling deputies could know.

Hardmun turned, his muscular arms still pinioned. He glanced at each of the deputies holding him. Bill Glasser, with his long, stringy, yellow hair and dusty bowler hat; and young Arch Tobler with a face full of red pimply blotches. Their broken-toothed grins stared at him like the faces of death.

Hardmun wanted to remember these men, all of them, as he drove straight into hell.

Capstin yanked viciously at Hardmun's chin, pulling his face forward.

'Feel good, does it?' he laughed. 'Looks all natural, it does. Like you was made for it.'

'Gonna hang,' Glasser cackled. 'Gonna hang.'

Hardmun felt a trickle of warm liquid down his neck, thick and heavy. Capstin's eyes lit up like a child's with a new toy. He wiped his fat, pig-like hand across Hardmun's neck and pulled away to show a streak of blood. For a moment Hardmun feared the sheriff would taste it. Instead, he simply wiped his paw clean across Hardmun's face.

'Gotta be careful, boys,' the fat sheriff bleated. His deputies giggled like little girls. 'Don't want our boy to die afore he dies.'

They all laughed now and Hardmun could stand no more. He spat into the eye of Sheriff Capstin.

Capstin yelled, 'You dog!' as he clawed at his eye. Hardmun wished he still chewed tobacco. Perhaps then he might have put out the sheriff's eye.

The deputies froze, uncertain, terrified. In the deadly silence that followed it was Hardmun's turn to laugh.

'You're a pig, Capstin. Always have been. Our roads may be different, but there's more honor in one of my kind than in any ten of yours.'

Holding a dusty bandanna to his eye Capstin threw his heavy fist squarely into Hardmun's belly. Hardmun had been expecting it, had stiffened for the impact. Yet the big sheriff had a lot of weight. He threw one hell of a punch.

Hardmun's knees buckled and with his collapse came more laughter from the deputies. He fought to control his stomach, afraid the tight noose would make him choke on his own vomit. He breathed tightly, willing air into his constricted chest.

'You're a highwayman, Hardmun, and don't you forget it! You rob people and that's agin the law. I'm the law, Hardmun, so it's you agin me. You see how it is.'

Hardmun looked up from the floor of his jail cell. Morning light was just now pushing through the barred adobe window. Another day in this sweatbox, he said to himself. One more day in this hell. Maybe it would be better if they just beat me to death.

'I see how you terrorize this little town, hiding behind a bought star,' Hardmun groaned.

Capstin's boot slugged into Hardmun's groin. The prisoner cried out sharply and tried to roll over. His body tensed from the pain so violently he felt a leg muscle pop. His stomach threatened again to void itself. Capstin's attack seemed to be a signal because the deputies joined in and began pounding hell out of Hardmun.

After the first few blows, Hardmun felt little. His mind sank into a numbing gray mist, cold at first but then warmer and comforting. He had no thought other than a desire to embrace death. Then darkness enveloped him.

When the blackness cleared, Hardmun found he was on the dirty floor and that the noose was gone from around his neck. He hauled himself up onto a rat-chewed cot, struggling just for breath. The sun had come up full and he was sweltering in the tight, airless cell.

Thinking at first that it was a rattlesnake, Hardmun was startled to find the hangman's noose in the cot. A rattlesnake of a sheriff had left it there to torment him.

And why not? Didn't he deserve it? This time, perhaps he did.

So many years on the loose, living life the way he wanted, not giving a damn about man, woman, or child. Only for his own flesh, his own belly.

He had lived well, so he thought. The sky for his roof, no time clocks to watch. Hell, he had almost forgotten how to tell time by means other than the sun or the stars.

Punching cattle meant slaving for forty dollars a month and grub. Town jobs paid even less and kept you out of the sun, burying you in some dusty room. Either way, you were working for another and not much of a man.

The highwayman's trail made life exciting and rewarding. You lived by rules, of course. Not the ones found in the Bible or even in the halls of the Capitol. But they were just as immutable. There was a code and Hardmun gladly stuck to it.

He would die for it soon. Sticking to the code would see that his gang remained free, for he had told nothing to Capstin, nothing to the judge and jury that had sealed his fate.

He deserved death, he told himself. You should have stopped Amos Turk, ended his life before he had had a chance to wreak his terrible, drunken retribution. You knew Turk was a mad dog and that he would bring about your death, he told himself. And now it has come true.

Yet the code remained. The murders committed by Turk, as the gang's leader, would go unavenged because

Hardmun would say nothing to the law. If there was one thing Hardmun regretted it was that he would not be around to punish Turk for his evil.

Those words echoed in his mind as he dozed through the day. His thoughts quiet again, he was amazed at the depth of his hatred, and of his desire to kill. He had not always been like this, and as he drifted into a fitful sleep he thought about the stages of his life and the circumstances that had brought him to the hangman's noose.

It had been a sudden spark, a bit of inspiration which had prompted Hardmun to lift his gun and carefully place the bore over the tip of the whiskey drummer's nose.

'Shut up,' he had told the portly, sweating man who had gone cross-eyed with fear staring at the large gun.

The two men had spent most of a day inside a hot, bouncing stagecoach. The hard wooden benches had numbed Hardmun's back and the whiskey drummer, who had announced himself as William G. Portis, had numbed his mind. Portis had wasted no time in bringing out a sample case and offering a taste to Hardmun, who refused. But as the grinding trip wore on and pain settled deep into his bones Hardmun knew he needed relief. Relief, too, from the incessant, mindless chatter of the drummer. Portis, by his own accounts, had traveled the depth and breadth of the 'Wild West' and had made the acquaintance of many fine personages, as well as those of lesser refinement. He preferred, he told Hardmun with a wink, the saltier among the species. With a knowing eye he saw Hardmun's discomfort and again offered a sample. Reluctantly, Hardmun drank. The brew was vile and he spat it out without swallowing.

Looking back on it, that might have been the moment

when he had thought to seek revenge on the fat salesman. The mindless drivel the man spouted was stupefying, but the taste of that whiskey would stay with him to his dying day.

'That, of course, is among our finest,' the drummer said with a grin. 'Meant for the stout of heart and stomach. Excellent medicinal uses, too.'

The stage suddenly lurched and the two men slid to the floor with a crash. When the coach came to a stop moments later they were yanked out and thrown to the dusty road. The driver was dead, the echo of a shotgun blast still hanging in the dry air. Two men with bandannas covering their faces were up in the driver's box, working free a small tin chest that had been bolted there. On horseback were two other men, their faces also covered. They held guns on Hardmun and the drummer, but their attention was focused on the job of freeing the tin box.

One of the riders cast an appraising eye over the captives and lowered his rifle so the barrel pointed directly at Hardmun's head.

'You ain'ta gonna be no hero, air ya?' he asked.

Hardmun shook his head slowly, watching the man with an intent glare.

'Not me.'

Eventually the tin box was freed and the bandits rode away, but not before driving off the coach team. For a long minute after the riders left, Hardmun did not move.

Already on his feet, the drummer went to his sample case and drank from a bottle of his own wares. His face puckered and he shivered involuntarily, but he drained the bottle.

'Sir, that is the closest I wish to come to death for a very long time. Why, those brigands treated us foully. Well, of course,' Portis said with a catch in his throat, 'these aren't the worst men I've ever run up against. Did I tell you the time when I met Flag Wardrup?'

Ignoring Portis, Hardmun went to the coach boot, found a shovel, then turned and paced off about twenty feet from the road to dig a shallow grave. Portis spoke the entire time, sitting on a large rock to better observe the work. When he had interred the dead driver, Hardmun got his satchel from the coach and began walking down the road.

'Surely, sir, you do not intend for us to walk to our destination. Why, we must be twenty miles or more from. . . .'

And that's when Hardmun put his gun to Portis's nose.

'I don't intend for us to do anything, mister. I'm heading out after those horses. What you do is your business. But if you say another word to me, or trail me, you'll get right close to death, real quick.'

Almost as an afterthought, Hardmun reached into the man's coat and removed his wallet. Portis wasn't as flush as he had intimated but he had a small sheaf of folding money. Hardmun took one hundred dollars and left the rest. The drummer started to protest but a twitch of Hardmun's gun silenced him.

'Payment,' Hardmun said, 'For not killing you, drummer.'

'Is it a crime to be neighborly?' Portis squeaked, trembling.

'It is if you're a lousy neighbor.'

Down the road a mile he found two of the stage horses grazing. They were docile, easy to catch up. Hardmun fashioned reins from the rigging that had not been removed by the bandits, chose the sturdier-looking of the two horses, and hopped aboard.

He rode for several days, not seeing anyone. He ate what he could trap and drank from cool streams. Eventually he came to a small town where he traded his horse for another. He bathed and ate well and slept well, all at the expense of the whiskey drummer. He drank little, gambled hardly at all, so the money stretched.

It wasn't until several days later that he had caught a glimpse of himself in the window glass of a bank. The years had not treated him particularly well. He had spent so much time out of doors that the elements had chiseled away at him and scoured his face and hair. He looked older than his twenty-four years.

The most shocking part of the image was the look in his eyes. He seemed haunted. His eyes were black and empty and never seemed to be looking at anything in particular.

A wry grin played momentarily on his face. Now he understood why women had pulled their children close when he walked by; and why men either turned away, or lowered their hands to their guns.

He looked mean and he looked deadly.

Hardmun suddenly noticed a man inside the bank staring at him with panic in his eyes. The man waved toward someone. A woman screamed and dropped to the floor. Hardmun watched, fascinated by the strange ballet taking place in front of him, all of it surreal. A quiver ran through him and he felt a momentary thrill of fear.

A muffled shot from within the bank made a thumping sound and the window glass shattered. Hardmun threw his arms up to protect his eyes, turned, and tried to jump off the shaded boardwalk. He felt a tug at his sleeve, never having heard the second shot. Dropping to the street he stumbled and fell behind a watering trough. There was blood on his hands and his face was tender.

'Bank robber!' someone cried.

Instinctively, Hardmun drew his pistol and fired toward the voice. He heard a cry of terror and then the voice screamed for the sheriff.

'You idiot!' Hardmun yelled, scrambling to get clear of the bank.

Around him a murmur had gone up. His vision was blurry and he squinted to look about. He could see men and women standing tentatively in doorways and at hitching rails. Some of the men were inching their hands toward their guns.

'I'm no bank robber,' Hardmun said. He got to his feet, using a post to protect him from the man with the gun. Slapping his dusty hat back on he said, 'I was just taking a look at myself in the glass.'

From within the bank a trembling voice said, 'I've been robbed and I know what you bandits look like.'

'That ain't me, mister.'

The tension in the street had eased now that the gunfire had stopped. People began pressing forward. Hardmun looked around and the closeness of people made him uncomfortable.

'I'm leaving, friend,' Hardmun said, as he backed toward his horse tied at a hitching rail. 'And I won't be back.'

Down the street a tall man was working his way toward the bank. He had the look of a fellow ready for action, a man able to deal with trouble. The sheriff, probably. Hardmun wanted to be gone before the man arrived.

'Don't you listen to him, folks,' another voice called out. 'He's a thief, all right. He stole five hundred dollars from me and left me to die in the desert.'

Lifting into the saddle, Hardmun glanced around and

immediately saw the speaker. It was the whiskey drummer.

'Hold it, you!' the sheriff commanded.

Gun still in his hand, Hardmun fired a shot into the dusty street. The sheriff and the other men froze. Women screamed and rushed through doorways.

With a tug of the reins, Hardmun spun his horse then kicked it into a sudden gallop. Shots trailed him as he raced out of town.

His horse had no bottom and Hardmun knew a posse would quickly gain on him. He rode hard for two days, using the land to hide his trail, cutting back through ravines and canyons until he was sure he had lost any pursuit.

The animal was nearly spent when he spotted a small farm with two fine looking stallions prancing around a corral. He waited for night before slipping in and trading his tired nag for a strong, fresh horse. Leading the animal toward the gate he noticed a well-used saddle hanging on a post in the barn. He looked long and hard at the saddle, wanting it but not wanting to steal it. But he had ridden bareback for too many weeks since he had roped up the stagecoach horses, and he was tired of it. He took the saddle and left twenty dollars on the post. It wasn't a fair trade, but it was all he could do.

He rode for three more days, running a cold camp, ever searching his backtrail. He had seen the sheriff and two or three others in those first few days, far back and obviously not sure of the trail. But since he had taken the stallion he had seen no one pursuing him.

Eventually he risked a fire and the occasional gunshot as he hunted meat. He had ridden up into the high country where the air was thin and cold. Bull pines stood like sentries all around him, silent yet somehow disapproving.

The crackling fire offered him no comfort. He chewed the meat he had roasted but tasted none of it. He stared off into the darkness and saw no ghosts. He saw nothing.

This wasn't the life he had planned for himself. But as a boy, burned out of his home, running ahead of the screams of his mother as she fought off Union soldiers, he had never had the opportunity to choose his own life. His family dead, his home gone, and terrified beyond all thinking, he could only run.

Here he was, years later, still running. And he still didn't know why.

CHAPTER TWO

THE DEVIL'S OWN

Led in by Bill Glasser, a doctor entered the jail carrying a medical bag and wearing, despite the heat, a black frock-coat.

'I come to examine you, son,' he said, though he looked younger than Hardmun's thirty-one years. 'They say you slipped and fell.'

Glasser cackled as he opened the cell door, unconcerned that Hardmun would try to make a break for it. One look at Hardmun, his bruises and blood, and you knew he could barely move.

The doctor did not introduce himself, in fact he barely even looked at Hardmun. He moved mechanically as he pulled items from his bag. He applied bandages and stitched a larger gash with catgut. He used whiskey liberally on Hardmun's wounds, reawakening pain that had been numbed by unconsciousness, but never offered his patient any. He spoke once, and then only to complain about the waste of good whiskey and medical treatment on a man who would be hung the next day. His eyes avoided Hardmun's, not trusting himself to stay true to his Hippocratic oath.

For an hour the doctor applied his skills to Hardmun and for an hour after that Hardmun slept well. When he awoke again the sun was setting and the sky outside his window was the color of blood.

Arango had come to life somewhat now that the heat of the day was waning. Bloated and orange, at last the sun slipped below the craggy western ridge ten miles out of town. Then, like owls from their holes, the denizens of this hell-baked town pushed out of their cracker-box homes into a gathering gloom.

Arango had little to offer a man. Hardmun had always hated it and steered clear with a vengeance. He would not be here now but for the cruelty of Fate.

Men came into the street, drawn to the macabre beauty of the gallows. They joked in their fear, grateful they would not have to be the one to climb those steps, or the one to take that final, eternal step into darkness.

As night became complete, their fear grew. Torches were lit, voices were raised. Somewhere in the din Hardmun knew whiskey was being drunk heavily. They would come for him soon, wanting to send their personal demons into hell under cover of black night.

Despite the warnings of his inner voice, Hardmun had pressed close to the barred window. He watched with grim fascination the forming of the drunken mob. He should have stayed away from the window, kept silent and hoped they would forget him in their revelry. But Hardmun was a fighter. If he was to be tossed into hell at the end of a hangman's noose, he preferred to choose his own time.

He wanted to call out to the mob, challenge each fearful fool to come for him. He would take as many as he could with him. Some would die, that was for certain, and that would have to be enough for Hardmun. He was already dead.

'Looks like you might not last the night,' the sheriff said from a dark corner of the jail. He had slipped in unobserved. Now he slid into the small orange pool of light cast by a lantern on the wall.

The two other cells were empty, their rusting doors open. Capstin went into one of these, leaned back on the cot. He picked his teeth with a small knife, smiling like the devil.

'Would you die to protect your prisoner, Sheriff?' Hardmun asked with a wry wit he did not realize was in him.

Capstin laughed.

'Well,' he said at length, 'I'd do my damnedest, Hardmun. I'd sure do my duty.'

'Uh-huh.'

Hardmun turned back to the window. Weak firelight flickering from outside lit his face.

'You're gonna die, Hardmun. Whether it's that mob out there or the court 'pointed hangman, you an' the Grim Reaper's gonna be pals.'

Hardmun turned away. The truth of the sheriff's words cut deep into his brain. If only he could get out and find Turk. He never thought himself a vengeful man, or a righteous man. The Bible said the Lord alone called for vengeance, not man. Yet sometimes the hand of man was needed to enact the Lord's will. Hardmun had had no religion, he did not think himself qualified to speak of holy things. But he knew it was right for Turk to die, and right for him to do the killing. If not for Heaven or for the dead, then for his own peace of mind. He would be able to face death then with a calm resolve.

He just had to be free – somehow!

'Forget brooding, boy,' Capstin said, lumbering to his feet. 'I'll protect you 'cause I want to see you dance tomorrow morning.'

A sleepless night passed for Hardmun.

Then, before the first rays of a new day cut through town, Capstin kicked the jail door open with a loud crash. He came in smiling and leading a soiled priest by the collar. The padre wore vestments that were torn and dusty, and as ill-cared for as the man himself was. A stench of whiskey rose off his dirty clothing and poured from his mouth.

'Say a few words over him, Padre,' Capstin crowed.

'The hell with him!' the priest cried. 'Woman killer! You murderer of. . . !'

Capstin nudged the priest with a heavy elbow. The man quieted suddenly, pulled a dented flask from his hip pocket and drank from it. The sheriff then drew his heavy .44, cocked back the hammer, and pointed surely at Hardmun's head, smiling like a demon.

Sheriff Capstin was a black blob in the red glow of a setting sun when Hardmun first met the man. Hardmun shaded his eyes, squinting, trying to pick detail out of the rippling image on the horizon. He approached slowly, keeping his hands loose and ready, but away from the short carbine in the saddle boot. His well-worn Navy Six lay wrapped in oilcloth inside his saddle-bags. The thing's weight and the heat radiating from it from the desert sun had impelled him to remove it from his hip as he rode. Looking at the ominous black figure ahead he cursed mildly at his luck. Comfort had eluded Hardmun for so many years. It seemed that the moment something became easy, something else would knock his feet out from under him. Even the smallest relief from hardship had its consequences. Watching as the black figure shifted to bring a rifle up to glint in the relentless sun, Hardmun knew this man would bring him trouble.

The road was wide and the town – Arango, he would learn later – was little more than a collection of sand-scoured clapboard buildings wilting in the heat. Hardmun could have gone around the man, who became more distinct as he neared. But instinct told him the man in the road would be more dangerous behind him than in front of him.

Hardmun stopped his horse within feet of Capstin and, not knowing how to address the man, remained silent. They watched each other, neither moving. Capstin's eyes narrowed eventually, taking Hardmun in with a single glance. The hint of a canny grin pushed at the man's fatty jowls.

'Been watchin' you a while, boy,' Capstin said, licking at his teeth. 'You done kicked up quite a dust trail.'

Hardmun turned a little in his saddle to glimpse at his backtrail. Dust hung in the air behind him and stretched out in a long, thin line.

'Guess I did,' Hardmun said, his face wearing an easy grin. He could see that Capstin wasn't impressed.

'Thought you was riding in hard.'

'Nope,' Hardmun said. 'Just riding in.'

'Thought you was.' Capstin lumbered forward suddenly and the move frightened Hardmun's horse. It bucked and fought Hardmun's control. Capstin circled Hardmun, disdain playing openly on his face. When he came back around he again stood in front of Hardmun.

'I'm sheriff around these parts,' Capstin announced. 'And the welcoming committee, too.'

'Was that funny?' The sheriff's blubbery face had turned to granite. 'Was that supposed to be funny?'

'No.'

Capstin's body seemed to shiver as he calmed himself. Hardmun had been watching the white-fingered grip the sheriff had on his rifle, knowing he had made a deadly mistake. The grip loosened now.

'That's better,' the sheriff said, tossing the barrel of his rifle out of his hand a few inches and then catching it as it fell back into his palm. 'You see, as sheriff, I gotta watch what goes on in this town. Gotta see who's comin' and goin'. Not much of a town, by the looks of it, but I keep it peaceful.' He paused as if expecting comment. 'You understand.'

'Sure. I understand.'

'Trouble is met with trouble. Now, just what're ya here for? We don't get many visitors.'

'Thought I'd get me a shave and a meal and maybe a bed for the night. My horse is wore out, too,' Hardmun said flatly. 'I need to get another one.'

'You mean buy one.'

'That's right.'

' 'Cause if'n it's the other ya got trouble with me.'

'I can buy one. If I can get some in trade for this one.'

Capstin's eyes brightened. 'Well, I'm the only one hereabouts with any stock what to speak of. I can give you five dollars for that wore out nag, but you'll need another seventy-five to catch up a fresh one.'

Hardmun took a long, calming breath. He was being

robbed but he needed to get away from this town. He knew that deep within him.

'Sure. I've got enough for that.'

'Well, foller me!'

'Say, what do you call this town?'

'Arango.'

Hardmun shook his head. 'Never heard of it.'

Capstin's face darkened. 'No reason you should have.'

They got to the center of town where a springboard and two stout horses stood silently suffering in the heat. Capstin lumbered aboard and picked up the reins, pausing a moment as if expecting comment. Hardmun said nothing.

'I ride just fine,' the sheriff said defiantly. 'But I don't if I don't have to. It's a mite uncomfortable. For me and the horse.' He let out a guffaw, and Hardmun forced a grin to his lips.

Two miles outside of town they came to a small house that was leaning to the left. Corral poles had been fixed to the side that tilted in an effort to keep the place upright. Tied to these with rough native hemp were other poles that spread out into a lopsided circle to form the first of three large corrals, all of which were in surprisingly good repair. There were more than two dozen horses standing as if rooted in place, their tails flicking anemically. The oppressive heat caused their shoulders and backs to slump.

'They're all of 'em fine creatures,' Capstin said. 'Heat's got 'em low, is all.'

Hardmun looked over the animals and chose one. As he had been expecting, the sheriff commented that that horse was one of his best, and a favorite of his, too. It would cost another twenty dollars. Hardmun chose two others, getting the same response. Finally he paid the extra money and took the horse he had first selected. It was a strong-looking cowpony, an Appaloosa with a straight back and what looked to be a good bottom. This horse would take him far. And that's exactly where he wanted to go.

'I could maybe make you a deal on a new saddle,' Capstin said, fingering the worn leather that Hardmun had just removed from the other horse.

Hardmun swung the rig up on to the Appaloosa.

'It'll do me for the time being.'

'Sure it will. Say, you mentioned something about a shave and a meal. There's a fine restaurant in town where you can get your fill.'

Hardmun got aboard the Appaloosa. It was a steady animal and didn't fight him. But its head bobbed a little, as if signaling its readiness to ride.

'You own it, don't you?'

'The restaurant? Well, I do at that.'

'Thanks.' Capstin began riffling the gold eagles Hardmun had paid him. 'After you're done eating, drop by the Pig Whistle saloon for a game. The boys and I are usually there after sundown.'

'I might,' he said, but both men knew he was lying. Hardmun had nearly $300 in his pocket, and he wasn't about to lose it sitting in on what would likely be a crooked game.

The meal he ate that night was greasy and cost three times what it should. He ate only because he hadn't eaten much in the past few days. After supper he went to the general store and bought supplies for the trail: coffee, flour, salt, a couple cans of peaches, and salted meat. He thought to buy some biscuits from the restaurant but after his sour meal he decided to stick to his own cooking. The rail-thin clerk trembled when Hardmun tried to haggle him down to a reasonable price.

'I cain't,' he said, shaking. 'Take it or leave it, mister.'

Hardmun's room at the hotel, with its threadbare blanket and moth-eaten mattress, cost eight dollars, and by then he was ready to take his old Navy Six and start pistol-whipping folks. But they had no choice in the matter. Nearly every business was owned by Capstin, including the barbershop where his face was nicked five times getting a shave with a dull razor.

Boredom and the tinny noise of voices echoing through paper-thin walls enticed Hardmun out of his room despite his better judgement. He had earned his stake working five months on a Montana cattle ranch, and another two driving the herd to the railhead. He had moved on in the spring, taking odd jobs for room and board, wandering aimlessly. He had no plan, no need for one. But he felt a heaviness press in on him. He had no idea why or what caused it, but only knew that he had to keep moving.

That wandering had brought him to Arango.

The Pig Whistle saloon, next to the hotel, was little more than a hallway shoved between two buildings. Long and narrow, there was only room for a short row of tables opposite the compact bar. There was no mirror above the meager selection of whiskey, no paintings of nude women. At the back of the room were four more tables. Two of these were empty, one had a drunk lying across it, and the last was home to a sluggish card game. The men there seemed to be waiting for something, and when Hardmun entered their play became more animated. Capstin was there, holding court.

'Ya have something?' the bartender asked. The man was unusually tall and thin. His face was pinched like a sunbleached cadaver.

Hardmun ordered a beer and drank it warm. Arango was in the desert and now that the sun had set, the air had cooled. But inside the Pig Whistle the heat lingered. Everything was warm to the touch.

Other sounds came from the other side of a door at the back of the saloon. A woman screamed and then the sharp crack of a slap was heard. No one at the card table moved. The bartender shifted and began cleaning glasses.

Suddenly the door burst open and a short, disheveled man stumbled out. He was dirty and his hair and beard were matted.

'Damned whore!' he cursed, roughly touching his cheek even as he struggled to hold up his pants. There was a welt on his cheek and a trickle of blood.

'Told you she was a wildcat,' Capstin laughed. 'There's extra for the rough stuff.'

'Like hell.' The man spat, and then froze. Capstin had drawn his revolver and the barrel was pressed into the man's belly. Slowly the man placed a coin on the table.

'That's better.'

Pushing to his feet, Capstin went over to the drunk at the other table and slapped him a few times. The man groaned and with bleary eyes looked up.

'Your turn, Maco.'

Maco sniffed and wiped his sleeve across his mouth, then swallowed the last of the whiskey in his glass. He stumbled toward the door amid the laughter of the other men.

Before the door could close, a dark-haired woman, looking more like an animal than a human, ran out of the room and up to Capstin. Her dress was dull and gray, worn at the seams. She had a feral beauty but her teeth were half-rotted and she was scarred along her arms and on her back.

'Not another one of your drunks, Capstin,' she howled. 'Not again.'

With a smile still on his face he backhanded the woman and sent her sprawling across the drunk's table. She lay there for a moment, breathing rapidly, her back arched, catlike. Her fingers tried to dig into the cheap wood like claws. She spun violently on the man, but did not strike him. They stared at each other for long moments before she turned and disappeared through the door. The men laughed again.

'Well, there you are, traveler,' Capstin said, pretending to just now notice Hardmun. 'I told the boys about you. Come join us.'

Hardmun's stomach was churning – from the beer, from the miserable food, and from what he had just witnessed. Capstin was a vile creature, and every bit of Hardmun wanted to give the fat sheriff a beating.

Feeling trapped, Hardmun stepped over to the table. Capstin made introductions, and their names promptly went out of his head. They were all of them human wreckage, aligned with the powerful sheriff if only to save their own worthless hides. All except Capstin's deputy, Kurtzman. He was a wiry man with keen eyes and the blank look of a man who had killed and enjoyed it.

'Take a seat,' Kurtzman offered, his eyes flickering over Hardmun's hip where the Navy Six was strapped on.

They let him win a few hands without appearing too obvious, then began taking back his winnings with a string of steady losses. He'd win another hand, then lose a few more. When he had lost fifty dollars he stood up from the table.

'Trouble, friend?' the tight-lipped deputy asked. 'Things are going pretty well.'

'I'm down fifty, friend,' Hardmun said casually.

'Night's young,' Kurtzman replied tersely.

Hardmun nodded. 'It may be, but my back ain't. Been riding a wore out horse too long. Need to stand for a while.'

'What you need,' Capstin said, 'is a new saddle.'

'Could be.'

Hardmun moved away from the table feeling the hair on the back of his neck stand on end. That deputy was a bad one; he meant trouble.

Another scream emanated from the room beyond. The woman stormed out, throwing her hands in disgust.

'He is a pig!' she cried. 'You are all pigs.' She slapped Capstin and the sound it made echoed in the silence that followed. 'He is asleep, drunk, useless.'

Lifting to his feet, Capstin said, 'Then wake him up.'

'No! He is a pig!'

With a blurring motion, Capstin shot a fist into the woman's stomach. She doubled over so quickly she seemed to snap. Hardmun turned back to the table, his hands balled into fists.

'Don't, friend.' Kurtzman was on his feet too, his hand hovering over a gleaming revolver in a shining, slick holster.

The woman could not scream, but her eyes welled with tears as she gasped for air. Capstin held her by one arm, pulling to get her upright.

'Stand up or you'll vomit.'

Hardmun's stomach churned so much that he thought

he would vomit as well.

'Now, get your scrawny-legged carcass back in there and finish him.'

'I can't,' she said, her body shuddering.

Capstin had been doing a slow burn since the woman slapped him. Now his anger was ready to bubble over. Dragging the woman, he hauled her into the back room and slammed the door. Instantly the woman screamed. 'No, Capstin, I'll finish him!' Her words were drowned by another scream.

Hardmun watched, his body tensing with his own rage. Kurtzman by contrast stood relaxed on the other side of the table, the fingers of his gunhand waving slightly as if caught by a breeze. He was daring Hardmun, relishing the chance for the kill.

Ignoring him, Hardmun took a step forward.

'Don't,' Kurtzman ordered.

Hardmun pulled the Navy Six from his holster and fired in a blinding motion. The bullet slammed into Kurtzman's chest even as the gunman fired. Hardmun fired again and Kurtzman dropped, knocking over the table and showering the room with cards and chips. Stumbling to get out of the way, the other three men ran from the saloon. Hardmun heard a low moan and, turning, saw the whiskey-slinger clinging to the edge of his bar. Kurtzman's shot gone wild had killed the bartender.

Hardmun kicked in the flimsy door and found the woman dead, her neck twisted unnaturally. Capstin was lying on top of her, his pants down around his knees. He jumped at the intrusion, grabbed a nearby chair, and flung it at Hardmun. Fending off the chair, Hardmun didn't see the sheriff's fist rocketing toward him. The punch knocked him back into the saloon and over a table.

Capstin came out, slipping suspenders up over his thick shoulders. He saw the bartender motionless and glanced down at his feet where Kurtzman had collapsed.

'You're a murderer, son. I'll take real pleasure in hanging you. Killing a lawman is one thing, but a poor used-up woman. You'll swing for sure.'

Hardmun wasted no words. He leaped forward, caught Capstin by the suspenders and twisted the fat man even as Capstin sent another punishing blow to Hardmun's face. They fell to the floor together, Hardmun holding a death grip on Capstin. On his back now, with Hardmun sitting on his chest, Capstin was like a huge tortoise. Unable to right himself he began flailing. A wild look of panic lit his otherwise flaccid eyes.

Hardmun slapped at Capstin's fat paws, clearing the way for a powerful punch that sent a gusher of blood from the sheriff's nose. Stunned, Capstin's arms fell away leadenly. With every ounce of hatred he could muster, Hardmun pummeled the bloated face beneath him until the sheriff's eyes closed over with bruises and blood-welts.

A sound from outside jarred him to consciousness. He had lost all sense of time as he beat Capstin, and when he looked down at the sheriff he felt revulsion at what he had done. Yet he knew he had done what was right. Killing a woman, for any reason, broke every code by which he had ever lived.

Capstin deserved death, but Hardmun would not be able to deliver it. The sounds he heard were of men approaching. Angry men. The other card players must have gone for help, he realized. Slipping out the back, Hardmun let the night swallow him. He found his horse and climbed aboard. With a burst of speed he rode hard out of town. The hatred in him did not cool in the chill desert air. Whipping his horse, wind tearing his eyes he saw an image in the darkness, a picture he had carried with him for years. The vision of his mother, screaming, tortured, lingered in his mind for many, many miles.

CHAPTER THREE

HELL'S RIDERS

Strange emotions flooded into Hardmun as he stood looking down the barrel of Capstin's gun. He felt almost hopeful that Capstin would fire and save him from the wrenching pain of the hangman's noose. Fear he felt, and anger, too. He wanted to charge the fat sheriff and feed him the barrel of his own gun. He had no right to do what only the law itself could do.

Capstin, though, would not kill him, and after a moment Hardmun realized it.

Keys were jangled and the cell door opened. Hardmun never took his eyes from the sheriff's twin, watery orbs. He stared with hate and with a desire to remember his hatred as he marched into hell.

The deputies slipped into the cell now and tied a stretch of rope around Hardmun's ankles. Sheer torture it would be walking to the gallows.

Bill Glasser stood up, looking Hardmun up and down

strangely. He twisted his face comically and sniffed at the air.

'You mess yerself, boy?' Glasser asked, turning with a snigger toward Arch Tobler.

Hardmun slammed his elbow back into Glasser's gut. The deputy groaned loudly and vomited, then fell to his knees holding his stomach. Fumbling, Tobler drew out a long-barreled .44. Hardmun caught the boy's hand before the gun cleared its holster. He twisted savagely, around and back. A sharp snapping sound echoed in the tiny cell just before Tobler let out a shrill cry.

The .44 had fallen at Hardmun's feet. Reflex sent his hand toward it, but the crack and ricochet of a pistol shot stopped him suddenly. It was the survival instinct in him that stilled his hand.

Capstin stepped into the cell and kicked the fallen .44 away.

'Get out and go see Doc Harrow,' the sheriff told Tobler, who was whimpering like a small child in a corner of the cell. The boy got shakily to his feet and stumbled out of the jail.

Then the sheriff kicked Glasser in the butt with the side of his boot.

'Can you stand up, you moron?'

Glasser nodded feebly and pushed himself to his feet. He swung viciously, then, with a hand full of pistol. Hardmun saw it coming but could not duck out of the way quickly enough. The sharp sight caught him just under the cheek, drawing a ragged, bloody gash.

'All right, that's enough!' Capstin yelled. 'I want him to climb those steps under his own power. Just tie him and let's get.'

A very clear thought came to Hardmun then. It was time to die.

And where would Turk be? Nearby, to hear of Hardmun's death? Or had he ridden off laughing like a coward, loud and full of bravado?

There had been a time when he had almost enjoyed riding with Turk and his gang. The open road was so appealing, but there was no way to make a living without turning to robbery. For a time Hardmun had done well on his own, sticking up the occasional stage, breaking into stores, or robbing a post office. Petty crimes that netted him little profit but allowed him to stay free as the wind.

But pickings were small riding by yourself, and there was no one to watch your back. It was only a matter of time before he would be caught and go to jail. Or he could give up and turn to ranching or clerking in some dingy store. Neither alternative held any appeal for him. Joining up with Amos Turk's gang, accidental as it had been, had seemed the perfect compromise.

In general, Hardmun did not like other people, but with the men of Turk's gang he got along well enough, or at least that's what he had told himself. They each understood one another, had the same dreams, and the same need to stay free. The road of the highwayman was their way to fulfill that need. Remembering now, though, he realized he had never really called any of those men friend.

Quickly they had developed a reputation. The thunder of their approach on horseback, the lightning flashes from their swift guns, and the fierceness of their demands inspired the name Hell's Riders. Never did they take a life needlessly. Hardmun saw to that. Yet the fire with which they committed their crimes stabbed fear into the hearts of their victims.

Turk had been a clever thief, too, not simply a vicious

criminal. And because of this Hardmun found no difficulty in taking orders from him. But after Abilene everything changed. They had surrounded the noon stage ten miles out of town, covering every window with their guns. The guard's scattergun had been thrown to the dust, the men taken out and lined up behind the coach. The women, as Western custom demanded, were separated from their valuables but left unharmed. The entire operation had moved with smooth precision.

Then a ten-year-old boy stood up with a revolver as long as his arm and leveled it at Turk's back. Hardmun had a quick eye and a fast draw. His shot rang out, startling the horses. The boy cried out and fell into the road, holding his hand tight against his chest. There was only a little blood but two of his fingers had been smashed.

'That was one hell of a brave thing, son,' Hardmun said to the boy, helping him off the ground. The boy fought back tears and tried so hard to show hate. But he was proud and had a right to be. He had been the only man among them to stand up to the hold-up men.

'You leave him be,' one of the women snapped, pushing Hardmun aside to take care of the boy. She was a pretty young thing but the boy kept his eyes on Hardmun. They had shared something just then. Even at that tender age, the young fellow knew he had stared into the face of death and had come away a winner.

'Don't be too proud, son,' Hardmun said, remounting. 'There's more to being a man than holding a gun.'

The woman turned viciously and spat.

'You wouldn't know much about that, would you?'

Later at their makeshift camp, Turk came up and put a heavy hand on Hardmun's shoulder.

'You saved my hide, Hardie!' he said, then swung his

knee up into Hardmun's groin suddenly.

'But in this outfit you shoot to kill!'

The others – Tallock and Briar and Morgan and the rest – gathered round in a circle, their faces hopeful. Hardmun looked up and saw their widened eyes lit redly by the small camp-fire. They should have been running a cold camp just after the hold-up, but Turk always refused. He yielded to no man or posse.

The others wanted a fight and for a few moments Hardmun was ready to oblige. He pulled himself to his feet and saw that Turk had set himself, ready for a charge. Hardmun smiled inwardly. No, he wouldn't fight today. He was twenty pounds lighter than Turk, although more muscular and lithe, and he had just been sorely hurt.

'He was a boy, Turk,' Hardmun said.

'If'n he can point a gun and shoot at *me* then he's man enough to die. Or do you got other ideas?'

The men pressed around them, willing a fight to start.

'If that's how you want it, Turk, fine. But you do your own killing. Just don't you ever lay a hand on me again.'

Hardmun pushed through the circle of men and went to his bedroll. Disappointment hung in the air thickly. Several of the men threw disgusted glances his way. Not to fight was not to be a man. Then, too, not a few of those men would have enjoyed seeing Turk get a sample of his own medicine.

A volatile man, Turk was. An eager friend and a rabid enemy, sometimes both in turns. He was not a man to be crossed and Hardmun knew right then that things would have to come to a head sooner or later.

In the darkness of his cell, Hardmun realized he should have killed Turk when he'd had the chance. Hardmun didn't want to lead the gang, though, and killing Turk would have put him in charge. Like a wild pack of dogs, or some primitive tribe, the men would have turned from the corpse of their fallen leader to the new chief. Hardmun wanted none of it and so let his chance slip by.

Glancing out the window at the gallows, he thought again of his life, as a man is wont to do under such circumstances. He thought of the few good things he had done and felt a pang of remorse. He refused to give into despair, though. He was getting the end he deserved. He had had his chance at redemption and, ultimately, failed.

Strangely, the time alone on the trail in the years before meeting Turk were easier for him than the days he spent in towns. Although he never settled, constantly on the move, the vast wilderness enveloped him with a sense of belonging and purpose – and the feeling of home. Of course his purpose was to keep out of the way of Indian war parties and to hunt for food. But that was enough. He could wander where he wanted, ignorant of all boundaries, living free.

Occasionally the comforts of town would beckon to him. He would ride in to some wagonstop or mining town to enjoy a shave and a hot bath, a change of clothes, a little whiskey. But he didn't enjoy the people. Too many of them were dirty and mean and territorial, suspicious of all newcomers. Strangers, he decided, tended to bring out two things in people, one good and one bad. For some the arrival of a stranger meant hearing news from other parts of the country, catching up on the world, and simply engaging a new conversation. For others – for too many others – a new arrival was occasion for mistrust or manipulation. Women saw him as a way out of their small lives, men saw him as a threat to what little they owned.

Over the years he came to hate going into towns, and avoided them as much as possible.

So the irony of finding himself one warm spring day standing in the middle of a nameless place in Oklahoma and actually enjoying the sights and sounds of a peaceful community was not lost on him. He boarded his horse, intent on a shave and bath, but found the barbershop closed. Most of the businesses were closed and the lone dusty street through town was quiet.

A soft breeze brought to him a hint of honeysuckle and the sound of voices singing. Hesitating only a moment, he turned away from the saloon and walked to the end of the street where a white church stood gleaming brilliantly in the sun.

Heads lifted as he entered the church and found space at a pew. Hardmun wasn't wearing his gun and had his hat in his lap, so he didn't attract too much attention. The preacher paused for a second, nodded a greeting, then continued with his sermon. There were a few giggles from young girls sneaking backward glances at him.

The place was quiet and cool and he enjoyed the simple act of sitting still. Mechanically he rose with the others, sat with them, and bowed his head as each gesture came in turn. The words spoken by the preacher, though, were indistinct, nothing more than a pleasant buzzing in his ear. It startled him when the service ended.

Hardmun filed out with the others. As he approached the front door, the preacher reached out and shook his hand. He was a strongly built man with short, wavy hair as white as snow. He was an outdoorsman, too, his face ruddy and worn by the elements. He could have been a rancher or a sailor, if not for the white collar peaking out of his black frock-coat.

'We're glad you could come,' he said in a melodic baritone voice.

'You speaking for the congregation, Father, or for God?' Hardmun asked.

'For God, of course.'

Hardmun let a wry grin creep into his eyes. 'You speak to him often, do you?'

'God is always pleased when one of his children comes home for a visit,' the preacher said, taking no offense at Hardmun's jibe. 'As for speaking to him directly . . . I haven't had the pleasure. But I have heard his echo in many things. I'm Matthew Ruffner,' he added, extending his hand again.

Hardmun shook hands again. 'Well, I thank you just the same, Father, for the sermon.'

'It's pastor. I'm not Catholic.' Hardmun turned away, walking slowly toward the far end of the street and the hotel. Ruffner followed with an easy stride. 'You're newly arrived, aren't you.'

'Rode in this morning.'

'Most men right off the trail visit a saloon, or perhaps . . .'

'Didn't have the urge, preacher.'

Reaching out a hand, Ruffner took Hardmun's arm and the two men stopped.

'I don't blame you. Visiting a saloon right after church would be a bit unseemly. But perhaps you'd care to join me on my front porch for a beer.'

'Beer? On a Sunday, preacher?'

'On a warm day such as this beer can quench a little better than lemonade, don't you think?'

'I do at that.'

Ruffner smiled broadly and began leading Hardmun

down the street again. Past the hotel, the town broke up into scattered buildings and homes. One of these had a gate and a neatly maintained garden, and a short porch with a table and two chairs.

'I make my home here so I must walk to the church,' Ruffner said, pushing open the gate. 'It's less convenient, but I'm always out among the people, the pious and the sinners both. My job, my jurisdiction, reaches beyond the church fence.'

Ruffner disappeared into the house, returning in a few moments with two glasses and a tall, brown bottle. The men sat and the preacher poured beer, rather expertly, Hardmun thought, into the stubby glasses.

'In the navy,' Ruffner said, 'I believe they call this a short beer.'

Sniffing at his glass, Hardmun remarked, 'In the navy they put saltpeter in the beer.' About to drink, Hardmun had a sudden thought and concern flitted across his face.

Ruffner laughed. 'No need to worry, son. I told you. I'm not Catholic.'

They drank quietly for a few moments, Ruffner waving to the occasional passer-by. Hardmun told him of his plans in town, a little of his own background, leaving out his criminal pursuits, talking despite himself. Ruffner made conversation easy, and Hardmun found himself hungry for it. The preacher wanted nothing from him and wasn't suspicious of his arrival. It had been a long time since Hardmun had felt comfortable in a town.

Ruffner poured more beer.

'Careful there, Preacher,' Hardmun teased. 'You'll end up needing a liquor license.'

'The path to the devil, son, is in excess. Everything in moderation, the Bible tells us.'

'Does that include killing, Preacher?'

Startled, Ruffner looked hard at Hardmun. 'Is that what you're really here for, son?'

Hardmun smiled. 'No, Preacher. It's like I told you, shave, bath, and some supplies. That's all.'

'You don't have to go so soon. There's work to be found here. A man can't live alone his whole life.'

Hardmun turned away, his jaw tightening. 'I wouldn't be much use as a store clerk,' he said gravely.

'Perhaps not. But the blacksmith is looking for a strong man to help him, maybe even apprentice.'

'Shoeing horses, Preacher?'

'It pays, and you won't have to hunt up every meal. And once a week at the church, the ladies have a supper. It'd be a free meal.'

The conversation faded, but pleasantly. Hardmun stayed with Ruffner that night and in the morning made his goodbyes. Spending much of the morning on his chores, Hardmun found himself procrastinating over his departure. He had been avoiding the blacksmith all day but decided to have the Appaloosa reshod. The smith was a large black man with biceps half as round as beer kegs. Wiping his gigantic hands on a stained leather apron he reached to shake with Hardmun.

'Pastor Ruffner told me something of you,' the man rumbled. 'I'm Coates. Jeremiah Coates. And I'm a free man.'

Hardmun nodded. 'I'm a Southerner, Mr Coates.'

Coates's eyes narrowed. 'You're honest, at least. I expect we won't have any trouble.'

'I do not expect that at all.'

With a simple nod from Coates Hardmun was hired. They had barely spoken, but the two men understood each other. Despite himself, Hardmun felt comfortable with the blacksmith and was glad to have work.

He shoed his own horse that day, and learned a little something about shaping shoes. Coates had a room at the back of the shop which he let Hardmun use to sleep in.

In very short order, Hardmun became part of the community. He attended the church suppers and, every now and then, the Sunday services. He ate regularly, worked hard, and after some months began giving thought to courting the milliner's daughter. On occasion, the old restlessness would creep up his spine making him irritable or anxious. But the emotion was subdued, muted. He would turn to the fire and the anvil and bang out horseshoes or a scythe or a wagon buckle, and drive away the restiveness.

The following spring several men came riding into town. Hardmun watched them approach slowly, their eyes casting about the town, flint-hard and cruel. They dismounted outside the livery stable, leaving their horses, then split up as each went in a different direction. One of the men came to the smith.

'Boy!' he called.

Coates, bellowing a fire, didn't even look up.

'You deaf, boy?'

In the shadows, Hardmun realized that he had become still. He felt a shiver run through his body as a burst of fear swept over him. These men were on the hunt, and they were looking for men.

'Damn it, boy, I'll shoot yer black ears off,' the man growled, drawing a long-barreled revolver.

Coates's eyes lifted to take in the shadowy man framed in the doorway.

'How can I help you?' Hardmun said, suddenly stepping forward. At that moment he was more afraid of what Coates would do than what might happen to him.

The man turned away from the blacksmith and thrust a Wanted dodger at Hardmun. The face on the worn paper could have been anyone.

'We don't know his name, but he's a big fella, rides a paint, been seen around these parts.'

'What's he done,' Hardmun asked.

'Robbed a stage around here last year.'

'Anybody hurt?'

'No. He fired a couple of shots, knocked off a feller's hat, but that's about it. Got away with about two thousand dollars.'

Hardmun forced down the bile rising in his throat. He remembered the robbery, but he had taken less than $200.

'There's a five-hundred-dollar reward, so keep your eyes peeled.'

The man spun on his heels and strode away.

Later that night Hardmun went to the saloon were the riders had congregated. There were five of them and they had taken a table at the back of the room. Hardmun ordered a beer and stood at the bar drinking it, trying not to glance over at the men.

'Hey, blacksmith,' one of them called.

Hardmun took a deep breath, picked up his beer, and walked to the table. He was being foolish, he knew, daring these men to recognize him. But the terror he felt seeing these men come to town had driven him a little mad. It had brought out a terrible guilt in him. He believed part of him was hoping to be recognized, and he trembled at the thought.

'You remember something about that dodger I showed you?' All of the men were so similar Hardmun wasn't sure he was talking to the same man from that afternoon.

'No. Sorry.' The others turned to look at him, casting no more than a rough, appraising glance over him.

'Five hundred dollars in it for ya. Cain't make that working for no darky.'

His throat tightening, Hardmun replied, 'Like I said, I don't recognize him.'

They were ignoring him now, intent on their cards. With a shudder of disgust, Hardmun turned from them and bumped into a small man coming up to the table.

'I do apologize, sir,' the man said, brushing beer from the front of his vest.

Hardmun froze. It was the whiskey drummer he had robbed what seemed like ages ago. The man, Portis, looked up and smiled warmly.

'No hard feelings, heh? Besides, it looks like I got the worst of it.'

'No. No hard feelings,' Hardmun said, and returned to the bar. The whiskey drummer hadn't recognized him. Glancing back toward the table he saw that the others had made room for Portis. All six of them ignored him.

Over the last year Hardmun's criminal past had begun to fade from his memory. He wanted to laugh now as the word redemption came into his thoughts. Without knowing it, he had sought a new start in life. And now he had one. He had found redemption. Not in the church or with a woman, but under the simple veil of anonymity. Unrecognized, he had become a different person, free from the crimes that nagged at his heart.

His hands tied in back of him now, Hardmun was led out of the Arango jail into the glaring morning sun toward his end. Long shadows fell on the dusty street, none longer than the dark image of the gallows at the center of town.

The men of tiny Arango had gathered early, their bravery returned now in the light of day. They jeered and threw stones. A few of the two dozen or so men drank from dirty whiskey bottles. It was a holiday.

Hardmun paused sharply. Beneath the gallows and mounted atop his gray gelding was the colonel. Old, stern, his gray mustaches severe and pointed, he sat proudly and defiantly. The old man had chased the Turk gang all over the badlands in those few final weeks. He was the only one to see the job through. Now, for the both of them, the end was here.

CHAPTER FOUR

THE UNFORGIVABLE ACT

The colonel wore no uniform and had given no name, but Hardmun always thought of him as a military man. A Southerner, too, with those mustaches. The man, though well weathered, had a youthful appearance that belied his snow-white hair. He sat his steel gray mount – a giant beast near sixteen hands high – as if steel was shot through his spine. His eyes were dark and deep. There seemed to be no mercy, no quarter possible within the man. His pursuit of Hardmun and Turk's gang proved that. He was a dynamo that would not stop, couldn't be driven off, couldn't be killed. At the end when he captured Hardmun he was alone. He had cared for the outlaw's wounds, got him well enough to ride, and then brought him back to Arango. Hardmun had no doubt that after the hanging he would ride out again in search of the rest of the gang.

Through Hardmun's convalescence the colonel had spoken barely a word, and offered no information as to his background. Even his accent was mild and resisted definition.

Hardmun walked to the gallows.

'Your end is here, son,' the colonel said, remaining mounted.

Smiling weakly Hardmun said, 'Yours, too.'

The briefest of nods from the old man indicated his acknowledgement. 'As far as you are concerned, yes. You still don't care to say where your murderous friends have gone to?'

'I don't rightly know. But I wouldn't say if I did.'

Hardmun found that he was very calm in the face of the uproar surrounding his execution. He blotted from his mind the noisy rabble that had collected behind him. Men drunk with whiskey to bolster their courage, women secretly relishing the violence, and children fascinated by the spectacle.

The colonel nodded deeper and said, 'Then I suppose I'll have to keep on looking.'

'I wish you very good fortune, sir.'

Capstin pushed heavily at Hardmun's shoulder and directed the condemned man up the stairs. It was hard going for Hardmun, his feet kept close by the restraining rope. Catcalls sounded with each step.

As Hardmun scanned the gathering dully, a woman standing alone on the boardwalk outside the barbershop caught his attention. She was plainly dressed in a tan gingham dress, dark-red blouse and soft boots. Her face was soft, too, creamy, as if she had not spent much time in the sun. She was quite beautiful, he thought, except for the harshness of her eyes. They were a bright green, darkened now as she stared at him with such hate. No, not hate. Determination. It was as if, with just the thought of it, she was willing his death.

Atop the gallows the priest waited together with a black-hooded executioner. The priest was mumbling some words sourly, waving with his hand and vaguely making the symbol of a cross. Sheriff Capstin pulled out a black hood and moved toward Hardmun.

'Got any last words, boy?'

Hardmun glanced down at the colonel.

'I'd like to know your name, sir. Before I die.'

The old man remained stoically unmoved, keeping silent. Perhaps it was fitting not to know the man's name. Hardmun believed he had already received more courtesy from the colonel than he truly deserved.

Riding as an outlaw, Hardmun's mind had never given rise to such thoughts. There had been a world for the taking where only the strong survived. He had been strong and so he took, although he had never believed in hurting others. Now he wondered if he hadn't been weak, preying off those who had fought to make their meager, though honest way.

After Abilene and the showdown at the camp, Turk soured. He drank more, beat his men, scarred his horses with sharpened spurs. Constantly he turned on Hardmun, trying to bait the man into a final showdown with guns. Though larger and stronger, Turk cared little for fighting men of strength, and he preferred guns to fists.

Hardmun steered clear of Turk's wrath. He rode without complaint and took his share which, after a few weeks, had shrunk considerably. He asked about the cut and Turk laughed. Hardmun had been reduced to watching the horses on most of their jobs and that kind of work didn't pay much.

A fire was building in Hardmun. He would have to confront Turk and then one of them would die. Hardmun, though, did not want the responsibility for that on his hands. Not back then.

They rode to Mexico that winter, ahead of a posse from Drago Flats. Turk had made his first mistake in a long time. They had robbed a train and now had Pinkertons as well as railroad detectives on their tails. The job had netted only $2,000, and the baggage man and engineer had been killed.

Briar and Turk had gone to the baggage car, Tallock and a new kid, Graiwer, stayed with the lead car. Graiwer was a wild-eyed child whose gunhand shook, though not from fear. The boy simply itched to use it. From his post with the horses Hardmun suddenly heard two shots. He needed little else to know what had happened, and what awaited them in their future.

Turk sensed it also. He forgot his enmity and, fear clinging to his features, asked Hardmun for advice. Hardmun said they had to go to Mexico now, for a while. So they rode.

Half-way through Arizona they spotted the posse. This was no home grown group of straggling riders. These men rode with purpose and with skill. Very little dust followed in their wake. Only by chance had Hardmun spotted them. Turk wanted to turn and fight, but Hardmun persuaded him otherwise. These men were too good.

The gang rode more carefully after that, running cold camps, posting guards. After a few days of tense riding they had come to the ridge of a narrow range. From there they could get a clear look at those following.

That was the first time Hardmun had seen the colonel. He knew then that they were in real trouble. The man rode with authority and dignity, and he appeared as tireless as Atlas. The others deferred to him in all things. He commanded with an unpretentious confidence that was apparent from even a distance.

The border came and went and still Hardmun advised continuing on. The old man had put a fear into him that he had never known. Such constant pressure, though, took its toll on Turk. His anger grew, he drank constantly now, and he became hotly resentful of Hardmun to whom the men were now turning for guidance.

Eventally, at Tinto, Turk called a halt. The posse had not been seen in days and Turk believed they had turned back. The men believed it, too, wanting to be shed of their fear. So they drank and shot at chickens and kissed many willing *señoritas.*

Hardmun didn't argue. The ride had worn on his nerves, too. A blackness seemed to be folding over his eyes and his heart. He had known for a long time that he was doing things he really didn't want to do. But for so many years he had gone along aimlessly. He had never really found a dream to hitch to. Torn from his home, set on a lonely road as a youth, he had had no time to think about what he wanted out of life. Even now he didn't know what he wanted. But he knew what he didn't want.

He ignored the women and the bitter whiskey, ate little, and kept out of lighted areas. He was like a wild cat, sensing danger, prowling the small town, his eyes always peering into the black night surrounding them.

His vigilance paid off. Two nights later the raid began. Expecting it, Hardmun was able to see a band of men sneak into town, crouched low and guns drawn. There were only six men, though. Turk had been partly right, most of the posse had turned back.

Lazing on a dirty couch set out in the town square, entertaining two willing *señoritas,* Graiwer saw the shadowy movement, too. He leaped to his feet, drunk and dazed, and began shooting at every suddenly thundering shadow in the darkness. He was cut down in a hail of bullets.

Hardmun avoided the gun battle and went for the horses. He saddled as many as he could find, then led them out behind the main hacienda. Tallock understood when he saw the horses and rounded up the others. Under covering fire, the gang got out of Tinto and headed back north.

All during the frantic ride north something nagged at Hardmun. For miles he could not imagine what his mind tried to tell him. Then, as they reached the border, he knew. He had not seen the colonel in the raid. And the colonel was not a man to give up.

Try as he might, Hardmun could not persuade Turk to find another route back into the States. He knew without a doubt that the colonel would be waiting for the gang, with the rest of the posse.

Turk was furious at having been bearded in his den. Like some wounded animal he ran with fear and little thought. To tell him of his fear was to invoke a mindless, violent rage that would see much blood spilled. So Hardmun rode and hoped; hoped that in the vast desert expanse of the border the colonel and his calculating crew would miss seeing them.

Such hopes died in an onslaught of lead. Guns from all around them opened up their red-orange maws and began spitting hot death on them. The gang scattered in the thunderous chaos of the attack. They had walked into a narrow, short draw surrounded by high walls. Only a minute of easy riding would have brought them through safely. The place had looked so innocent as they approached.

Now their horses reared and screamed at the echoing explosions of the posse's rifles. Hardmun pulled hard at the reins of his beast and brought it under control. A bullet struck his shoulder. A glancing blow that frightened him more than hurt.

He broke through the draw and out into the open flatlands. He rode hell-bent, and doubled over to present a smaller target. By some miracle his horse had not been shot out from under him.

Out of rifle range he pulled up and turned. Others had made it out, bloodied, terrified, but alive. Turk was with them. His terror, though, showed like a crazed fire in his eyes, a fire of pure evil. He was furious and ready to kill anything.

Through squinting eyes Hardmun spotted the colonel on the plateau above the draw. The old man had made a mistake. They had planned to kill off every one of the gang in that draw and had not foreseen that some would escape. Now they would need many long minutes to walk their horses down from the plateau to renew the chase.

Tallock and Briar and Morgan had all of them made it out of the draw with Turk. His closest men, the cruelest of the bunch.

They rode like men fleeing the gaping maw of Hades. To Hardmun's mind that was exactly what they were doing. He had no love for these men any more, only the need to get away from them. The pressure of pursuit had brought their true colors to the surface and it sickened

Hardmun. Yet he knew he had to ride with them still. There was safety even in their reduced number. Later there would be time to turn away from these men – and perhaps away from the life he had been living.

Two days of hard riding got them no further from the trailing posse. From jagged hills they would occasionally be able to spot the lazy cloud of dust rising far in the distance. The posse did not gain, but neither did they falter.

On the third day – the horrible, cursed third day – they came upon the small farmhouse. It belonged to a homesteader with grand ideas of being a rancher. The wife and baby child were alone, the rancher gone to tend his tiny herd.

Turk skidded to a stop outside the front door of the house and thrust himself into the water trough. He came up gasping, drenched in cold sweat and sun-warmed water. The homesteader's wife, a game if somewhat frail woman, came running outside, her baby crooked in one arm.

'Heavens! Are you all right?' she said to Turk.

Looking past her to a meager corral, Turk saw two horses. He turned to Morgan and said, 'We'll take them.'

'But there's only two, boss, an' they don't look so sturdy.'

'They's fresher'n what we got. We'll take them and switch off if we have to.'

He started for the corral but the woman stepped into his path. She was about to protest when Turk backhanded her, sending mother and child to the hard, dusty earth. The baby started crying as a tiny gash welled red on its small head. Turk paused over her, his face boiling with fury.

Hardmun leaped from his saddle and struck Turk with a staggering right and left. Turk backed off, dazed. The big man shook his head and swung around toward Hardmun as if confused.

'You damned cur!' Hardmun cursed. 'Leave the woman be. Let's just take some food and go.'

Hardmun turned to the woman, the baby's cry a piercing thing in his ears.

'Sorry, ma'am,' he said simply.

'Them's the only horses we got, mister,' she said, trying to comfort the baby. 'You can't strand us.'

'Shut the damned kid up!' Turk bellowed. Hardmun turned to see Turk nearly wild now, blood-red in the face and shaking. Evil was in his eyes. But more than that. He was desperate to kill something, to strike back at anything within reach.

Hardmun knew then that Turk wanted him dead.

In an instant Turk's gun was up. Hardmun, wounded in the shoulder, flinched, but his muscles did not respond. He felt a stabbing hot pain cut into his side, then another stab into his right leg. The world became a red blob for him after that as he crumpled to the ground.

Through a dark haze, Hardmun watched Turk as he pulled the horses out of the corral. The woman protested, crying, tugging at Turk's shirtsleeve. Her words were silent in Hardmun's ears. The world was silent except for the throbbing sound of his heart, the rushing of blood in his ears.

Turk hit the woman twice more but she kept getting up. She kept trying to stop the animal that was Turk. But the animal would not be denied. With less thought than it would take to swat a fly, he finally swung his gun hand around and fired. The bullet pierced child and mother both. Hardmun tried to rise and call out, but his body wouldn't respond.

Through the dark shroud that was growing over his eyes, Hardmun saw the woman and baby fall. The baby was dead and the woman screamed her silent terror. Turk, smiling horribly, leveled the gun and fired again and again. Finally, the woman, torn up by heavy lead, lay dead in the dust.

Hardmun swore feebly, shaking as he again tried to rise. His one thought was to kill Turk, to slaughter the animal. But he could not move and soon he slipped into oblivion.

Time passed quickly for Hardmun after that. Revived and healed, tried and sentenced, he was to die for the crimes of another, crimes that he knew in his heart he should never have let happen. Unforgivable crimes. His overriding regret was still that he had not killed Turk. Now it was too late.

The colonel did not look at Hardmun, did not offer his name, and Hardmun understood. He allowed himself to be shoved back over the trap door, watched as the noose lowered over his head. Hood in hand, the sheriff came close to Hardmun.

'You are a vile dog, Hardmun. I will be so glad to watch you die.'

'If you're what this world holds for the future, Capstin, then I am glad to be going.'

In the distance thunder roared and Hardmun thought it inappropriate that the heavens should rain on account of his passing.

Keen animal that he was, Capstin paused, his eyes widening. He turned and tossed the hood aside.

'Grab iron, men!'

There was a frantic slap of leather but it came too late. The thunder roared around Gepson's livery stable at the far end of Arango and rode into town on horse's hoofs. The animals were driven remorselessly at breakneck speed carrying gunslinging riders.

They moved like the wind, a blur to the eye. Shots cracked almost soundlessly beneath the deafening roar of their charge. Onlookers ran from the street, screaming.

Hardmun had a moment frozen in time when he could make out one of the riders. It was Turk! Turk had come to rescue him!

CHAPTER FIVE

GILT RESCUE

Hardmun had only a moment to register the amazing thought. Had Turk some deep-buried sense of loyalty? Or was it animal instinct? He was a craven coward underneath the bluster, of that Hardmun was certain. Perhaps the beast knew his master, after all.

Sheriff Capstin fired several shots at the whirlwind that was Hardmun's rescue. Seeing the futility of it, he turned and leveled his pistol at Hardmun, the outlaw's neck still held by the loose rope.

'I'll see justice done, boy!' the sheriff screamed above the din. He turned toward the hangman, but the black-hooded man had jumped from the gallows and run to safety.

Somewhere in the mad volley of shots, lead struck Capstin and he crumpled to his knees. Unable to move his gunhand, a spark of intelligence suddenly flashed in his misting eyes. He glanced down at the trap door release and smiled weakly. Then he pushed his fat body up and slumped onto the lever, throwing it forward.

Hardmun, hands and feet tied, could only brace himself. The trap door swung down, the rope losing slack instantly. Hardmun yanked his head back with a snap, hoping to catch the rope not on his throat but on his chin. Severely, the hemp cut into him beneath his chin. He had kept the noose from snapping his neck or, what would be worse, choking him to death slowly. But if he could not somehow wriggle free he might still asphyxiate.

Pain seared the back of his neck, his muscles tight to the point of bursting. He felt blood and sweat trickling down his neck. He needed no more wounds, he knew, and each drop of spilled blood weakened him that much more.

Then miraculously the rope snapped loose and he fell. Lying there in the dust, it took him several seconds to realize that a well-placed bullet had severed the death cord.

Bedlam reigned on the lone street of Arango.

Men ran for the cover of water troughs or open doorways. Many had not worn their guns this morning and ran to find them in a panic. The few women in town for the hanging shrieked, dodging raging horses and flying lead.

In their dash through town, the gang doubled back, then raced through again, creating wild confusion. Dust rose in a swirling opaque mass. To fire into it might mean the killing of innocents, so the townsmen with guns held their fire unless given clear shots. Turk and his gang offered few such opportunities.

Hobbled, his ankle throbbing from the fall from the gallows, Hardmun limped his way into the street. A horse drew up sharply, kicking stones and dust. It was rawboned, sallow Morgan.

'Climb up!' he roared, reaching a hand down for Hardmun.

A shot splintered one of the gallows' support beams behind Hardmun. He needed no other encouragement to drag himself up across the flanks of Morgan's horse. Barely had he settled when Morgan kicked the animal hard and rode out into the center of all the confusion.

There were more gunshots now as the dust swirled up and away in the hot breeze. Hardmun glimpsed one of the riders – a man he did not know – fall to the street dead. He saw others, too, drop, red flowers blossoming on their shirts. So much destruction, he thought, as Morgan pointed his horse out of town. So much death just to save one man.

Away from Arango the gunshots continued. Hardmun managed to turn his head but could see no pursuers. Then he saw a small remuda of saddled and barebacked horses, all of them riderless, being herded ahead at full gallop. Somehow Turk had rounded up most of the horses in the small town and driven them away. Pursuit, he knew, would not come on foot.

After a time, the remuda of stolen horses was abandoned and the gang regrouped. Hardmun was thrown across the back of another animal and carried along like fresh-killed game. He asked to be untied and was ignored.

His rescue was indeed a gilt one. From the hangman's noose to the assassin's bullet, he told himself. Riding stomach down against a hard saddle, he thought he would have preferred being shot or having his neck snapped to this endless torture.

They rode until nightfall then stopped to make camp. Turk brazenly called for a fire to be lit. In the still, clear air it would be seen for many miles. Turk had no fear of pursuit, though. It would take many precious hours for the townsmen to gather up their horses, if it could be done at all. A full day would be lost.

Hardmun's hands were untied and he was seated in front of the fire with a plate of beans, dried beef, and hard bread. Coffee was given to him, but all of it in silence.

He saw that Turk had added a few men to his gang since last they had seen each other, now several months ago. One of the fallen men had been new. The others, three Hardmun believed, were young ones eager to make names for themselves. They blazed with excitement over their own bravado at having rescued Hardmun. There had been a lot of men who had fallen along the way. Somehow Turk always found more hardcases to replace them as they died. So many had been killed, and yet Turk still lived. The injustice of it ate at him.

Turk came forward at last and stood over the rescued man. Hardmun did not flinch, did not even pause in his slow, casual eating.

'I suppose I should thank you, Turk,' he said, spooning beans into his mouth.

'Ya think so.' Turk laughed. 'No. Ya don't. Ya don't 'cause ya know I got no love for ya, Hardmun. Maybe now yer guessin' just what I got planned.'

'Better make it quick, then. You're going to have a posse on you soon.'

Turk shook his head with authority. 'Took care of that.'

Hardmun shoveled more beans into his mouth and tore off a chunk of bread with his teeth. He realized something at that moment. The colonel had been seen nowhere once the raid on Arango had begun. And he had been mounted.

'Are you sure you got 'em all?' Hardmun asked, a light grin playing on his face.

'What the hell are ya grinnin' about?' Turk demanded,

kicking Hardmun's plate of food from his hands.

Turk then turned away and walked off into the shadows. All around him the celebration of the raid continued, men drinking, firing off occasional pistol shots. Even the sad-faced Morgan smiled a few times and tilted back a bottle.

But it was Turk that interested Hardmun. The man was frightened. Not because of something he knew might happen, or even suspected might happen, but simply because he did not know what would happen. For Turk it was some nameless thing in the darkness of his own mind coming for him. Hardmun recognized the terror of cowardice in Turk's eyes. He knew that, come the time, Turk would fight like a madman powered by that fear.

'Shut up, ya boneheads!' Turk yelled suddenly. 'Ya'd think we's a bunch of women at a dance. We got a job to do tomorrow.' He turned and looked across the fire at Hardmun, his face relaxing for a moment, grinning. 'We got us a traitor to kill.'

Hardmun knew what Turk would be like the moment he first laid eyes on the outlaw's Wanted poster. A deep sense of foreboding had rippled through him that day.

Hardmun had been off the owlhoot trail for more than a year, working as a blacksmith's apprentice, when the itch to travel overcame him. He had become proficient at the smithy, spending hours bent over a heated brazier and anvil, banging a five pound hammer on glowing iron. Coates had taught him much about the profession and the large black man took pride in his student.

On occasion Hardmun would deliver what he had created to the farmers and ranchers who had ordered goods or tools. He would ride the Appaloosa slowly, enjoying the sky above him and the vast grassy expanse all around him. This was freedom, Hardmun thought.

Soon, he didn't need an excuse to ride out into the country. It was then that he knew he would be moving on. He felt a deep sadness at that, because he had found a measure of peace in town. But he had never tried to make much of a life. There were several women with whom he kept genteel company, all of them pretty and capable and wanting more than he could give. He would look at each and could not imagine life with them. While in general liked by the town, he had made no lasting friends except, ironically, Henry Walthers, the county sheriff.

The two had met on the ride back from one of Hardmun's deliveries. Seeing the man's star sparkle in the sunshine, Hardmun became instantly tense, wondering if someone had recognized his face in that Wanted dodger. The sheriff introduced himself and swept a brief glance over Hardmun, inspecting him thoroughly. Seeing Hardmun carried no gun, the sheriff relaxed and this in turn eased Hardmun.

'Been looking for a man,' Walthers said, handing a folded paper to Hardmun as they rode. He was a tall man, sure in the saddle, with broad shoulders and whipcord arms. He smiled easily. His face was youthful but worn by the elements, like so many men in the West.

'Still haven't found that fellow, huh?'

Confused, the sheriff said, 'Just started looking for this jasper. He's a mean one.'

Hardmun unfolded the paper and looked at a frightening image. The artist had taken great care in drawing detail around the close-set eyes and the scars on the man's roughly bearded face. The name at the bottom of the dodger read Amos Turk and a $1500 reward was being offered.

'Different fellow,' Hardmun said. 'Some riders came into town last year and showed a different dodger.'

'Oh, that one,' Walthers said with a nod. 'Those were Rangers. But they figure that jasper left the territory.'

Walthers came to town several times in the next year, and Hardmun met him each time. Quickly they became friends, an event whose irony was not lost on the former outlaw. He liked the sheriff's easy going manner and his dedication to keeping the peace. After his distasteful experience with Capstin, Hardmun found it refreshing that a lawman wanted nothing more than to do his job well. They could have been lifelong friends.

But Hardmun had decided to leave, driven partly by his desire to wander and partly because he didn't want to disappoint Walthers. With a sinking feeling, Hardmun suspected his past would catch up with him and shame him in front of his friend.

Coates was waiting for him the morning he saddled his horse and loaded supplies into his saddlebags. In the smith's huge hand was a small canvas pouch that jingled as he moved.

'Some unpaid wages,' he said, stiffly.

'I've been paid, Jeremiah.'

'Not all of it. You take it, ya hear?'

Hardmun reached out to take the pouch. In a lightning move the big blacksmith gripped Hardmun's hand and held it firmly.

'You ride with care,' he said. 'Don't want to hear no stories about you.'

Hardmun nodded, not for the first time having some doubts. He was throwing away hard-earned redemption, and for what? He had no plan or purpose, no destination. He didn't even want anything except the sky and emptiness around him. Well, he thought a bit sourly, that's why they call it wandering.

'Tell the preacher. . . .' he started to say, but his voice trailed off. He really had nothing to tell the preacher. Nothing that his leaving wouldn't say for him.

He rode out across the grassy valley, the Appaloosa heading west. Hands at several ranches saw him from a distance and waved, not really able to tell who they were greeting. It didn't matter to them. Alone, with nothing but cows to talk to, these men savored every human contact. Hardmun came to a range of low hills by nightfall and camped. The following day he went up into the hills and began working himself toward a canyon passage he had heard some of the men in town talking about.

Riding west was the only plan he had. He needed time alone in the wilderness, away from lighted lanterns and tables with chairs and the polite but repetitive nods of hello to people he met every day on the street. He was not built for civilization, or what passed for it. Already, the tension in his body and mind was beginning to ease. There was a slight pang of guilt for not having bid farewell to the preacher, and another of regret for not having being able to live up to what the town had wanted him to be. But these were dull aches, hardly noticeable as he rekindled his loving acquaintance with the wild.

For two days he traveled over rocky passes, most of them narrow and dark. Eventually he came to a forested tableland and found a game trail through the densely packed woods. He camped by a stream and caught fish and roasted them on a spit. The area was cool and pleasant, and there was much food for the taking. He could have stayed there for days, yet the pounding of his very pulse seemed to urge him onward.

He had been in the wilderness for more than a week when the smell of woodsmoke drifted toward him. He reined the Appaloosa up short and caressed the animal's snout to keep it from making noise. He didn't dismount, preferring the height advantage should an attack come. After a moment he heard the sound of voices speaking softly. The words were indistinct and they seemed to flow in and around the trees making it impossible for him to pinpoint their origin.

There was a strange sense of foreboding in him. He had no desire to see people and so attributed the dark feeling in the pit of his stomach to that emotion.

Cautiously he turned his horse onto his backtrail. He would give these people a wide berth, if necessary. Perhaps they were Indians – a war party roaming – or trappers hunting for pelts. It didn't matter who they were, Hardmun wanted no part of them.

Another horse snorted in the distance suddenly and drew a nicker from Hardmun's mount. Reining up, Hardmun listened. The voices had gone silent. After a moment he heard hoarse whispers and the rustling of underbrush. Deep down he wanted to make a run for it, but the Appaloosa had turned and nickered again. Hearing voices approaching, he made a split second decision.

'Hello, the camp,' he called.

A rough voice called out, 'Who are you?'

Hardmun stepped nearer. In the shadows of closely packed pine Hardmun could see two pale faces staring out at him. He let a sigh of relief escape through his lips.

The men came out into the open wearing guns. One

had a rifle up to his shoulder, the other a shotgun held in two grimy hands. They were haggard looking, these two, with drawn faces and dirty clothes. Yet their eyes were beaded and sharp, like animals caught in a trap.

'Just travelin' through,' Hardmun said plainly.

'You lost?' the one on the left asked. He was taller, broader in the shoulder. He constantly wiped his hand on his threadbare shirt.

'Just travelin',' Hardmun repeated. 'No place in particular is where I'm heading.'

The other one ducked his head to look down Hardmun's backtrail.

'You with anyone?'

'Nope.'

'We've had some trouble,' the second man said. 'Rustlers.'

'I ain't a rustler. Where's your herd?'

The man jerked his head over his shoulder. 'There's a clearing out a ways. We got maybe a couple hundred head. Not much, but it's ours. Lost a few of them dogies in the woods as we were settling down for the night.'

'Rough trip?' Hardmun asked.

The first man wiped his hand again as he tried to straighten his clothes.

'We've seen some action.'

'Well,' Hardmun said, 'I'll leave you fellas to it, then.'

'Whyn't ya light for coffee and beans. Wouldn't mind jawin'.' This was the second man. He spoke plainly but there was something behind his words. There was a danger to this man that Hardmun couldn't define.

'Thanks,' Hardmun said. 'But I'd better mosey along.'

'You ain't headin' no place special. You said so yourself. Light and join us.'

He didn't exactly point the shotgun at Hardmun, but the weapon did move, if only slightly. Hardmun was now within its range.

Nodding, Hardmun nudged the Appaloosa forward to where the two men had tethered their horses near a clump of junipers. The two men mounted and rode behind Hardmun until they were out of the forest. Then they trotted up to flank him.

Ahead was a cattle herd, spread out for the evening in a glade of long, golden grass. There was a small ribbon of a stream behind the animals, and only a few of the beeves were drinking. The others had settled, their tails flicking lazily. Two riders moved through the herd slowly, rocking easily in the saddle. A light wagon sat near the stream its tongue pointed west. A fire was crackling and a large black man in a soiled bib apron tended the pots hanging over it.

Hardmun and his escorts pulled up and dismounted. The cook cast a sideways glance at them and looked about ready to say something but didn't. His mouth was tight and hard.

'Found a wanderer,' the taciturn fellow said as he wiped his hands on his shirt.

'What's he want?'

'Why, coffee and beans, of course,' the other said, smiling. He turned and stuck out his hand. 'Name's Parkins.'

'Hardmun.'

'Well, you sure got yerself a hard handshake, fella.'

'You shouldn't be here,' the cook said. 'You get on back.'

'Now, Ramos, we's being hospitable, ain't we? Them dogies will keep.'

The cook scowled. 'Dogies?'

'Lost in the woods,' the taciturn man said. 'We've been looking for them.'

'Then get back to it.'

Parkins's eyes narrowed. 'Coffee and beans,' he said, coldly.

Hardmun hadn't believed Parkins's story about looking for lost cattle, and this last exchanged proved him right. A tingling sensation began working through him. He desperately wanted to leave.

The cook brought a plate of beans and a slab of bread, then poured coffee into a tin cup. Hardmun thanked him and began eating. The others got their own food and sat close by.

'My pard,' Parkins said, 'is called Tulsa. Only – and this is funny – he's from a place what they call Sheboygan. Ain't that something?'

Tulsa wiped his hand on his shirt again, but said nothing.

'The boss is still out riding the herd, but he'll be in soon enough. Say, you looking for work?'

'No. I'm just wanderin'.'

'Well, a man could always use a stake, am I right? We'll make out all right with this herd and you could earn a few dollars. Of course, if you got all the money you need. . . .'

Parkins let his words fade as an innocent smile hung on his tight lips. Hardmun had paused in his chewing for only a moment, feeling his stomach turn.

'Wish I had some money,' he said.

'Well, then, you could use the work.' Pleased with himself, Parkins settled back and finished his meal.

Already hidden by low hills and trees, the sun began fading. After a while, a rider approached the camp from the herd. He was a big man but featureless, a silhouette in the waning light. He stepped down then stopped short seeing Hardmun. Instinct made his hand twitch toward the big gun at his hip. Then his eyes darted out at the edge of the campsite with suspicion.

'What is this?' he growled.

Parkins got up and, brushing grass from his pants, went over to the newcomer.

'Got us a stray, boss. A rider passing through. Needs dough, though, so I thought there might be room in the outfit for another hand.'

'He alone?'

'Looks like.'

Stepping into the ring of firelight, the boss asked:

'You any good, mister?'

For a moment Hardmun's gut froze. He recognized the face in the red glow, the cruel deep set eyes, the grizzled jaw, the flattened nose. He had seen that face on a Wanted dodger a month ago. This was the outlaw Turk.

'Good enough,' Hardmun said, 'but I think it's better if I move along.' He stood, conscious of the hard eyes on him.

'Ya don't want no job?'

'Came off a job a few weeks ago, I'd just prefer riding free for a while.'

Turk stepped closer. 'Ya ain't a rustler, are ya? No. I could tell if'n you were. Ya ain't no Injun and ya ain't law, either.'

'I told him we could use a new hand,' Parkins said.

Turk jerked his head around. 'Shut up. I decided that.' There was something dark in Turk's eyes as he turned back to Hardmun. Something blackly gleeful. Turk was toying with an idea that pleased him. 'Ya'll stay the night anyway. Ya don't want to be alone in this country if'n you don't have to be. We seen a couple of war parties already. Don't wanta lose yer scalp, heh?'

'No,' Hardmun told him. 'I don't.'

Hardmun spent the night in his bedroll by the fire with the other men, but did not sleep much. He had wanted to get his Navy Six out of his saddlebags but he was always under the watchful eye of one of the gang. He managed to get his knife, though, and held that out of sight through the night.

The men were up long before the sun. Ramos stoked the fire and banged pots as he put on coffee. Grumbling, the others rolled out of their blankets into the chill air.

A sudden gunshot slapped into the firepit splattering sparks high into the air. Turk spun toward the bedded-down cows and cried out that the herd would stampede. Another shot ricocheted off the wagon wheel's rim, the bullet clipping Tulsa in the arm. The man screamed and cursed and starting throwing lead around wildly.

In the darkness they could hear the sudden thunder of hoofs as the herd, woken from sleep, panicked and ran.

More shots cracked and someone yelled to douse the cookfire.

Hardmun ran for his horse but before he could leap into the saddle Turk grabbed him by the back of his shirt and yanked him to the ground.

'Worry about the cattle later, we need to get the shooter.'

The big man took Hardmun's arm and half led him, half hauled him into the early-morning darkness. Glancing back, Hardmun could see the others scattering, too.

Dropping down behind a large rocking, Turk said, 'I think there's only one, the fool.'

'He had the drop on you,' Hardmun reminded breathlessly.

Something ragged crossed Turk's face.

'On us, traveler. He figures yer with us. And ya'll have a hard time convincing him otherwise, if'n he lives, that is.'

'I'm not killing anyone, even if he is a rustler.'

Turk snorted a laugh. 'Ya will when it comes to it, mister. And that ain't no rustler. That's a lawman.'

In the dim glow of the dying fire Turk could see his words had not shocked Hardmun. The ragged line grew.

'Figured ya had us figured out.' Suddenly Turk jabbed his gun into Hardmun's belly. 'There's only one way out for ya, mister. What'll it be?'

'I can't fight without a gun.'

'I ain't that stupid. Ya get a gun when I can trust ya. Now get out there and stop that lawman.'

Hardmun felt the gun prod him again in the belly. It was obvious he had no choice. Rolling slowly away from the rock, Hardmun used the tall grass to hide in as he crawled toward the forest's edge. The others in the gang, secure in the darkness, had been returning the gunman's fire. For a few minutes, the sound had been deafening. But now there was only sporadic gunfire.

Hardmun wanted no part of this fight, and he wanted nothing to do with Turk and his men. As he reached the forest he thought of not stopping, simply disappearing. He owned little, and by dumb luck had kept his pouch of money on him and not in his saddlebags. He could leave the Appaloosa behind if it meant his safety. The others might try to hunt him down, but he was willing to gamble on that. Besides, if they escaped the lawman, they would have to round up their scattered herd, leaving no time to pursue a stranger.

Hardmun slipped up behind a close stand of pine and got his bearings. He could see the dying embers of the camp-fire, and beyond it the wagon. There was the rock behind which he and Turk had hidden. The muzzle flash of a long rifle spat out from behind the thick trunk of a willow which stood near the stream.

There was no answering shot. The lawman had gone silent.

Hardmun worked his way around the stand of pine, stepping over fallen branches, easing his way deeper into the forest. He forced his mind not to think of distance or speed. If he did that he would be overwhelmed, for he moved slowly and he would have to go far to escape.

Sporadic shots rang out. Turk called out tauntingly behind his rock, but there was no reply.

'Hold it, you,' a voice whispered. Hardmun felt the cold muzzle of a revolver press into his neck. 'Drop your gun.'

'I haven't got one,' Hardmun said, his heart pounding in his chest – not from fear, but from recognition. There was something familiar about the lawman.

'I said . . .'

His words were interrupted with the crack of a tree branch. Instinctively, Hardmun threw himself backward at the lawman just as a shot cracked. The lawman grunted as the two men fell to the ground and tried weakly to free himself using one arm. His other arm lay flat and useless on the ground.

'Good work, Hardmun,' Parkins said, running up to them. He cocked his gun and pointed at the injured man.

'Hardmun?' the lawman said.

There was little light by which to tell facial features, but the man's voice was unmistakable now. This was Sheriff Henry Walthers.

Parkins ignored them and leveled his gun. Hardmun made an instant decision. He grabbed Walthers's gunhand, swung it up toward Parkins and pulled the trigger. Parkins groaned even as he pulled the trigger, sending a slug punching into the dirt beside Walthers's head.

'Hardmun,' Walthers said, 'I can't believe you're in with this gang of rustlers.'

'Quiet!'

'I'll see you hang for this, even though it turns my stomach.'

'Shut up!' Hardmun pulled back then sailed his right fist sharply into Walthers's chin. The lawman collapsed, unconscious. Quickly, he dressed the lawman's wounded arm then scooped Parkins up over his shoulder and left the forest. The others saw him and came out from their hiding-places.

'What's this?' Turk asked as Hardmun dropped Parkins's body to the grass.

'Parkins got plugged, but I got the lawman.'

'With what?' Turk asked suspiciously.

Hardmun lifted Parkins's shiny revolver. He held it easily, aimed at nothing in particular, yet the muzzle of it never strayed from pointing at Turk's gut. The gang leader nodded toward the gun.

'Ya know how to use that thing?'

'Yes. I do.'

A feral intelligence came into Turk's eyes. He watched Hardmun carefully for long moments, looking deep into the man. He saw something that made him smile. The cold, ragged line that crossed his face made Hardmun's stomach churn.

'Well, as long as ya got the lawman,' Turk said, his voice a bit taunting. 'Guess that makes ya one of us.'

'I'll take my chances alone,' Hardmun insisted.

'Ya don't want to do that.' The tone was unmistakably

ominous. 'Besides, I'm down a man. Ya'll take his place. But we gotta go now. There'll be others that follow yer dead lawman.' Hardmun turned his head, glancing back at the forest. The sky above the trees was beginning to lighten. Soon it would be dawn. If they were found by a posse there would be no time for explanations. They'd all be gunned down or hung. 'Yer an outlaw now, Hardie, boy. Whether you wanted to be or not.'

The life he had known for the past year was truly gone now. He couldn't go back, and he knew it. He could never go back.

CHAPTER SIX

'DIE SLOW, YA DOG!'

Morning came swiftly, the sun blazing over the flat horizon with stabbing rays and instant heat.

Turk was awake early, anxious and excited. He roused his men with a gunshot that echoed endlessly in the still morning air. Hardmun, awake much of the night, did not move, feigning sleep. His hands and feet had been tied again after he'd eaten his meal and he had spent hours cutting at the ropes with a dull rock. He had nearly cut through them when Turk fired his shot.

Hardmun needed some more time but Turk kicked him in the ribs with the toe of his boot. Hardmun grunted and rolled over.

'Pick him up, boys. We got us a little exercise to do afore breakfast.'

The men were a haggard lot this day, heads aching and bleary-eyed. They moved with sluggishness as they saddled horses and gathered up their kits.

'Aw, let us get something in our guts first, Turk,' one of the new boys moaned.

'Case ya forgot, ya damned fool, we're still on the run. That posse won't wait around ferever.'

Obviously a plan had been made some time ago, for the men set about it now with all the economy of tired men. They pulled a coil of rope off one saddle and unrolled it to its full length. Then they took the ends and made heavy, careful knots around the horns of two saddles. First, though, they passed one end of the rope through Hardmun's legs. Any movement on that rope and Hardmun would be dragged along the ground by his feet.

Hardmun did not resist them. To do so would have brought heavy punishment down on him. He would need his strength for what lay ahead.

Turk surveyed the arrangements and nodded with pleasure. He motioned to the men to take to their saddles. Each of them was beginning to warm to what was to come. Eagerness showed in each man's face, a sadistic glee.

'Ya tol' that sheriff about us, didn't ya?' Turk said quietly, leaning down over Hardmun.

'You know I didn't.'

With the flat of his hand, Turk slapped Hardmun across the face.

'Ya lyin' dog! We've had men on our trail since we left that homesteader!'

'After you killed that woman and her baby.'

Turk smiled and nodded. 'She riled me something terrible.'

'I told no one anything about you, Turk. Not for any love of you, but because I want you all to myself. I'm going to kill you, Turk.'

The outlaw laughed at that. 'You don't kill, Hardmun.'

'You'll be the exception.'

'Well,' Turk said, backing away toward his horse, 'yer ghost is gonna have ta do yer killin', Hardie. 'Cause yer already a dead man. Ya just don't know it yet.'

The big man got on to his horse, checking the knot tied around the saddle horn. He turned in his saddle, following the rope with his eyes as it circled through Hardmun's legs and up to another saddle. Briar, soft and beefy, sat this horse, ready.

Smiling, Turk said, 'Die slow, ya dog! I want to enjoy this.'

With a wave of his hand, he and Briar spurred their horses into a gallop. Hardmun had dropped to the ground, bracing himself. But the first shock of being pulled almost yanked his legs from his hips. Stabbing pain shot up his back and into his head.

He lost his hat.

The hard desert floor cut into his shirt and into the seat of his pants. Sharp pebbles of chert cut little slices into his arms and back.

The gang rode a circle around Hardmun, whooping and cheering like Indians. Ahead, Turk and Briar pulled to a stop and steered their horses toward the east.

Hardmun had swallowed much dust. His eyes burned and his back felt raw. He had only been dragged a few score feet yet he felt weak as a child.

Turk turned in the saddle and gave a quick look at Hardmun. 'Still got some breath?'

He waited for no answer, putting spurs to his horse's flanks. The animal snorted and took off at a gallop, Briar only a step behind. They had spotted a stand of low, close-cropped *choya* and angled toward it.

Hardmun, bouncing painfully, rolled over onto his

shoulder. Fresh stabs of pain shot through his arm as he was dragged across the hard ground. The ropes that bound his hands were nearly cut through. Now they only needed a moment against the tough, rushing desert floor before they frayed apart.

The horses whinnied suddenly and stopped, stamping with their forelegs. They did not want to go into the patch of *choya.* Turk and Briar kicked at their animals cruelly, but could not get them to move through the sharp-spined plants. Briar suggested they flank the stand but the rope was not wide enough.

They turned again, now moving south, and dragged Hardmun past the *choya.* Hardmun was stuck with a few needle-like spines, though not badly. And now his hands were free.

He pulled himself up along his own aching body, reaching desperately for his legs. He could feel nothing in his legs but a dull tingling sensation. Panic sliced through him with thoughts he dared not contemplate.

Turk and Briar galloped on. The others laughed at Hardmun's attempts to free himself, waving their hats and cursing profusely.

When the riders paused again to change direction, Hardmun gathered up a length of rope. He turned his body to face forward then held on for dear life as the horses charged off again.

Several of the gang fired off some lead now, shooting into the air. One rider decided to take careless pot shots at Hardmun. The bullets struck close, spitting dirt and pebbles at the dragged and tortured man.

The knees of Hardmun's pants were rapidly being torn through. He needed to act swiftly. He twisted his legs, hoping they would respond to his command, and pressed the rope that bound his feet against the rushing ground. The effort to keep his feet steady was enormous; every muscle in him strained.

Turk and Briar stopped and turned. They conferred quickly then headed for the *choya* again. This time they would run close together then swerve to avoid the patch. Hardmun would be whipped around and into the sharp plants.

Frantically, Hardmun beat his boots against the ground. Blinking a glance back at his feet, he saw the rope fraying strand by strand. He glanced forward then, seeing the patch of *choya* rapidly approaching. If he was thrown into it, he knew he would never come out alive. He was all but done in.

Just then he felt a snap against his boot and looked back to see a tattered loose end of the rope. Free!

Hardmun released from the rope and skidded to a stop a few feet from a clump of *choya.*

Sensing no danger, the others rode up laughing. Turk and Briar made a wide circle and walked their horses toward Hardmun.

One of the new riders, a skinny boy of about sixteen, hopped down from his horse and said, 'Wonder if he's alive!'

Hardmun had not moved since coming to a dusty stop. Not for any plan he had in mind but simply because he was too tired and pained to move. Now, as the boy kicked lightly at his arm, Hardmun realized this was his only chance for escape.

With a swat of his hand, he knocked the youth to the ground. The boy slapped frantically at Hardmun with one hand and sought out his gun with the other. Hardmun fell on him and wrenched away the revolver. Turning wildly he fired three times.

Horses bucked. Two riders were thrown. Another frightened animal butted Turk's horse. Turk had drawn his revolver and fired but the bullet went wide of its mark.

Hardmun rolled away and fired another shot. A man screamed and fell. He rolled under the feet of horses and the animals stepped high over him. By some miracle he was not stomped to death.

Rising to his feet, Hardmun saw the confusion he had created. He could not count the men or horses; he had no time. He threw himself across the saddle of a blood red mare and shot into the dirt. Terrified, the horse reared and then launched into a gallop away from the gang.

Shots followed closely behind Hardmun. The air was cut by a vicious sound as lead passed far too close for Hardmun's comfort.

He rode, lying straddled across the leather, holding on with only a semblance of strength. The mare rode like the wind, choosing its own direction, fear guiding its steps.

Hardmun wanted to rest, desperately needed to rest. But to stop meant death. A man like Hardmun did not welcome such a thing, and certainly not at the hands of men like Turk.

The thought of dying at the point of Turk's gun angered Hardmun. And in that anger he found renewed strength. He would live. He had to, if only to kill the beast that was Turk.

A supreme effort of will brought Hardmun around on the saddle until he properly, though wearily, sat the blood-red mare. Leaning forward to avoid the trailing gun shots of Turk's gang, he gathered in the reins. The horse knew it had a rider now, not some bouncing bundle of lifeless flesh, and galloped with greater speed.

Quick glances told Hardmun he was headed north.

Around to the west were lava flats, hard, black, and lifeless. To the east were high, rocky hills. Directly in front of him rose a wide expanse of craggy spires of red and black rock. Hardmun could see many crevices between the rising rock, many places to hide. If only he could reach them.

Behind him came Turk and his riders. They had fast horses. Surprisingly, the mare Hardmun had stolen was fast, too. Maybe he would have a chance.

A few hundred feet from the wall of craggy spires, Hardmun spotted a narrow pass that disappeared into a black shadow. He guided the horse into it. The mare seemed to understand what was needed and plunged between the walls of rock fearlessly.

Once inside, Hardmun slowed the horse to a walk. The walls closed tighter and rose higher with each step. Shortly, he found his knees were rubbing up against the pass walls, which had worn smooth with age.

For a few harrowing moments, Hardmun believed the pass would be squeezed down to nothing and he would be trapped with Turk not far behind. Then the pathway widened. Both man and horse breathed a sigh of relief.

Behind him Hardmun could hear the clopping of hoofs stepping carefully. Turk and his crew must have known they were sitting ducks in the tight pass. Hardmun could lie in wait around a corner and pick them off one by one as they rounded into his sight. But unlike Hardmun, they had forgotten he was almost out of bullets.

'Ya got nowhere ta go, Hardie!' came Turk's taunting voice. It echoed down the pass, bouncing from wall to wall, surrounding Hardmun. The psychological effect on him was greater than Turk realized.

'Come on back, Hardmun.' This was Tallock's voice, deep and menacing. 'We'll make it easy on you.'

Was there something else in Tallock's voice? Yes, Hardmun decided, remembering. Tallock did not like closed spaces. He never slept indoors, even when hotel beds were available. He'd camp outside of town and say he was the ace in the hole if the gang ever got into trouble. Yet they all knew this was a lie.

Hardmun remembered now. If he could just spook Tallock in these close quarters that might prove enough of a distraction for Hardmun to slip away. It might even be worth firing off his last bullets to see that proud, power-loving man turned to a frightened child.

Hardmun called out down the pass, 'Hey, Tallock! Careful to look above you. Some of them rocks don't look too steady. Be a shame if any of them fell on you.'

A useless volley of gunfire echoed down the pass and Hardmun knew he had succeeded, at least partly.

'See, Hardie,' Turk called out, 'nothing's fallin'. Not a damned thing!' But his words were meant for Tallock, and all of them knew it.

Ahead, the ground rose at a sharp angle. The hard-packed sandy surface gave way to solid rock. The mare took to the rising path almost immediately and kept a sure grip on what looked to be slippery rock. This one, Hardmun thought happily, is part mountain goat.

Pain had given way to numbness in Hardmun's body. Blood had coagulated on the cuts in his arms and on his legs making him stiff and slow moving. His hat gone, Hardmun knew he would not last long in the desert heat. He needed to stay in the shade, but the sloping trail was bringing him up to a sun-drenched plateau.

Before reaching the top, the trail leveled and widened. There were several other narrow draws, any one of which might be a dead end. Above, columns of bubbling rock, now frozen and solid, pointed into the mercilessly hot sky.

The thunder of hoofs echoed up the pass. A shot rang out and punched a chunk of rock to Hardmun's left. Twisting in the saddle, Hardmun drew and fired blindly. He could hardly miss in the narrow draw.

The rider fell against the wall, his left foot still jammed into the stirrup. Terrified, the man's horse charged forward. The man, unconscious or dead, bounced and scraped against the wall until the draw widened. Then he fell beneath the horse's feet, trampled. The horse kept running until it disappeared down one of the other draws.

'Keep sending them through, Turk!' Hardmun called out. 'One at a time.'

Turk yelled back, 'How many bullets ya got, Hardie? How many?' The man laughed heartily, the sound a ghostly echo in the canyon.

Damn him, Hardmun thought. He was right. Hardmun had but one bullet left.

Quickly he studied the blind draws that faced him. There were four. Any of them or all of them might lead nowhere. If he chose the wrong one he would die. And yet he could not go back.

A shaft of the sun cut deeper into one of the passes ahead of him than into the others. Perhaps that one ran all the way up to the plateau above him. It was only a guess, but the only one he had to make.

With a nudge the mare started down the draw. At first Hardmun thought he had made a terrible mistake. The path narrowed and dipped and broke off three times. Then it began to rise again and he knew he was on the right trail.

Softly he spoke to the mare. He had great confidence in the animal, and respect. It was a proud animal, much like a stallion might be. Strong and sure it continued to move. On any other horse Hardmun's life might by now be forfeit, of that he was certain. Providence, perhaps, had other plans for Link Hardmun, he thought.

Hardmun heard curses far behind him. The others had reached the point where the canyon broke into four. He heard Turk yell, 'Shut up, alla ya!' And then silence. They might all follow one trail, but it seemed more likely that they would split up.

Hardmun's trail peaked only two feet from the top of a wide plateau of gently rolling lava rock, blackened by the sun and time. Surely, the mare stepped out of the arroyo and up onto the baking, sun-drenched mesa.

Dismounting, Hardmun squinted at the glare of the morning sun on the horizon. He needed a hat. But what he really needed were bullets.

He checked the rifle in the saddle scabbard to find a new Winchester. The action held fourteen rounds. Hardmun smiled. He could set a fine trap now.

The saddle-bags held an even greater surprise – bullets! Two boxes of forty-fives. Hardmun quickly reloaded and poured the rest into his pockets.

Leaving the mare, he followed the gouged earth keeping away from the edges until the canyon opened wide below him. He moved cautiously so as not to make a sound. If he could find Turk and kill him, it would be over. The others would abandon the search, he felt certain.

But to kill a man. This left Hardmun uneasy. Turk had been right in his accusation. Mostly, anyway. Unless pushed to it and without any other choice, Hardmun would not kill. Certainly not in cold blood.

Too, there was the matter of his reputation. Being a highwayman was no smirch on a man's record, at least in some circles. Such a reputation showed him to be a man of action, to have an adventuresome spirit. A certain measure of respect might come to a man with that character.

Yet he had been accused of such a foul crime, no man would want his company ever again. To kill a man was one thing, but a child and its mother? In cold blood? Such a thing would haunt him for the rest of his life.

Protesting his innocence would avail him nothing. What else would a stone cold killer say? Hardmun knew then with clarity that he could not kill Turk. The man had to be brought to justice.

Crawling now, Hardmun edged up to the rim of the canyon. The ground was hot and very hard. The lava, millennia old, had solidified into a rolling, sometimes jagged mass of rock. Ages of wind and sand had worn much of it smooth, almost shiny. It held the heat terrifically. In his already weakened condition, Hardmun was not certain how long he would last.

Hoofs crunching on loose pebbles caught his ear. Leaning carefully over the ledge, he peered down into the canyon trying to spot the riders. His eyes needed to adjust to the darkness below. Soon he could make out one, then two riders. Neither of them was Turk.

Hardmun ran back in the direction he left his horse. Half-way there, by the edge of the canyon, was a pile of loose rock. He went to this and quickly began dumping the rock into the narrow pass. He heard horses below whinny with terror and men shout, followed by a couple of gun shots. The gang would move more cautiously now.

Despite the noise, the mare had not budged. Hardmun went to the animal and patted its neck. 'Good, girl. Steady now.'

Then he climbed back down into the pass through which he had come, a narrow space of ten feet not much wider than an arroyo. It was angled, though, and it widened as it descended, giving Hardmun a clear view of much of the canyon below. Crouched low behind a rock just beneath the lava surface, holding the rifle tight, he searched out the other passes that he had avoided on his way up. Turk's men would be down each of these.

The first two men he found easily. The passes they had ridden into had circled around, looping back to their starting point. Peering over the rock and down thirty feet, Hardmun could see the riders cursing their luck. A third man was further on.

A shot smashed the lava close to Link Hardmun's head. Unseen, two of the riders had come up out of another pass on foot.

Hardmun spun his rifle around and fired, dropping one of the men instantly. The other ducked back into whatever pass they had used. Hardmun levered off three more shots, hoping the short barrage of hot lead would keep the man from trying to be a hero.

Men called up from the circular canyon below. They fired, too, but Hardmun was protected by the rock. The gang scrambled to find cover. They were sitting ducks down there, and very afraid.

Hardmun retreated up out of the arroyo and worked his way back toward his horse. There were too many of them to take on now that they all knew where to find him. Weakened, bloodied, and broiling under the merciless sun, he could not last much longer. He had to save himself.

Rushing the gouge in the lava where the gang had surfaced, Hardmun saw the dead man but no one else. His companion had slipped back down a dark, narrow pass that curved treacherously around a spire of bubbling, frozen lava. Hardmun took the dead man's hat, a sweaty, flopping thing of brown felt. He took, too, the dead man's guns and gun belt. Scavenging from the dead was not Hardmun's way, but to abandon such things would bring his death all that much sooner.

Something caught the corner of his eye and Hardmun turned. A man was climbing up out of the circular canyon, clawing with bleeding fingers. He rose to the rim and brought up his six-shooter. Fascinated, Hardmun had only watched the man. Now he reached down to draw his weapon, seeing how late he would be.

A shot rang out and the man clutched at his spine as he tumbled back into the canyon with a scream.

Then, faintly, a voice rose from down inside the canyon.

'Round 'em up, men,' the voice said, softened by wind and distance. 'Link Hardmun will be among them.'

The voice belonged to the colonel.

CHAPTER SEVEN

DESERT ESCAPE

The sound of gunfire echoed out of the circular canyon as Link Hardmun made his way back across the black lava mesa to where the dead man had fallen. Crawling up to the edge, Hardmun peered down into the canyon and saw horsemen milling about, shooting into blind passages, and the colonel at their center giving quiet but forceful orders. Hardmun backed away from the rim and hurried to his horse.

He replaced the Winchester and mounted, whispering gently into the mare's ear. The brave animal had a healthy touch of fear in it, Hardmun thought with a smile. Yet it had not run off when the shooting began. For that, he was deeply grateful.

The gunfire stopped and Hardmun knew that the colonel, and whatever posse he was riding with, would next come looking for him.

Just then, he saw a rider come slowly up from the ground, silhouetted by the still-low morning sun. Like a demon rising from hell, the large black figure gained the plateau of lava several hundred yards away from Hardmun. Slipping from the saddle, Hardmun pulled the mare down onto the hot ground. The distant figure never looked his way but instead turned and headed into the sun. The shape was all too familiar – Turk!

Another rider came up behind Turk and then another. Three of them had managed to elude the colonel. They had obviously been down in one of the many canyon passages when the posse struck and, much like the pass Hardmun had chosen, this one allowed Turk an escape route.

Now the three riders slipped away, careful to keep their horses to a walk, not looking back. Hardmun was profoundly torn. Escape and life lay within his grasp. Yet Turk, the author of all his woes, was suddenly in reach and vulnerable. Law had meant little to Hardmun over the years; but justice was a thing in which he believed deeply. It was unjust that Turk would walk away, a free man. He had to be punished.

Hardmun mounted the blood-red mare again and set off to follow, at a great distance, Turk and his remaining gang.

The flat lava plateau offered no hiding place. Hardmun was exposed for all to see. He rode away from the canyons and the colonel's posse, ever mindful of Turk, now almost half a mile ahead.

Twice his horse crushed the thin veneer of lava over what had been a prehistoric air bubble. The animal stumbled but righted quickly.

Hardmun dismounted to guide the horse. He knew that there might be large areas of the thin lava, brittle and very dangerous. The holes beneath the veneer could be inches deep or they could drop hundreds of feet into a dark oblivion.

Turk might ride boldly and make better time than Hardmun. Or he might stumble into a great void and disappear for ever. Hardmun, though, believed the outlaw would survive for, he thought wryly, only the good die young.

He found it strange, as he picked his way toward the end of the lava plateau, to think of Turk as an outlaw. True, the man had acted the criminal in everything he had done, but so had he, Hardmun. He had traveled that road, committed the same crimes, and never thought himself a criminal. He had been a man, hungry and in need. Men such as these take what they need. It was the law of this Western land. The cities provided statutes for men to follow; the wilderness had only one law – survival.

And yet, what was survival without honor? This had been in Hardmun's thoughts for a long time. It was what powered him now in his quest to bring Turk to justice. That, and his personal guilt at not having stopped the man sooner.

The ancient lava field ended, sloping to a hard desert floor. Ahead, Hardmun could see a faint dust trail lifting into the sky. In his caution, he had fallen further behind the gang.

To the north were low, rolling hills, rocky and desolate, seemingly devoid of all life. Hardmun knew better, of course. The desert offered an abundance of life, much of it, though, hidden from sight. Up in these hills, too, would be *tinajas*, catch basins for rainwater. Some might be filled still, even in this heat.

Hardmun checked the canteen hooked to the cantle. It was full, but that would not last him long. If Turk and his men had the same type of outfit, they would soon be looking for water.

Keeping to the base of the hills, Hardmun kept Turk's dust trail in sight. He pushed his mare into a canter, hoping to make up ground. If the wind was with him, his own dust trail would rise up and disappear against the hills. With luck, Turk would not know he was being trailed.

He kept an eye open to his backtrail as well. The colonel was too shrewd a tracker to have been thrown off the trail by a maze of canyons. Yet, Hardmun could see no one following him. He thought it just as well, for his mind was filled with a singular concern.

Nightfall came and still Hardmun pressed on. The desert night was cold. He was glad to have stayed in the saddle, taking what meager warmth he could from the movement of the horse. He kept the mare to a careful walk as the night was black as pitch.

Toward morning he dismounted, removed the saddle, and rubbed down his mount with a clump of brown grass he found growing in the lee of a rock. Then he slept. It was a deep, purposeful sleep, and dreamless. When he awoke, the new sun not yet over the horizon, he felt only a little refreshed. There would be time enough for sleep later, he thought.

After hours in the saddle and a night on the cold desert ground, he felt stiff and achy. His body was terribly bruised. He had scrapes all over his back and arms and legs, and the scabbing blood cracked as he moved. He looked over his torn clothes and laughed quietly. He was a terrible mess, a fact he quickly ignored as he climbed aboard the mare.

As he rode, the hills grew and turned their face toward the west. The ground elevation rose. Hardmun could feel the air cooling around him. He kept sight of Turk's dust trail, closing the distance between them only slightly.

He was running out of water and knew that Turk would soon need water as well.

As the afternoon sun baked down on him, Hardmun saw the dust trail move into the hills and disappear. The trick that had kept him from being seen now worked against him. He had lost Turk's trail.

He rode hard then, pushing the mare into great, ground-gulping strides. She was a strong animal, and desirous to run. She took to a gallop with a natural eagerness.

Hardmun had been perhaps four miles back of Turk. He had wanted to sneak up on the outlaw, not give him the chance to prepare for an attack or to set up an ambush. Now, that no longer mattered. He must not lose sight of Turk.

After a few miles' hard running, he pulled up on the reins and brought the mare to a canter. He watched the hills closely, hoping to catch sight of the gang making their way up the hills. No luck.

He went further, then dismounted and led his horse at a walk. He needed close scrutiny and a keen eye to catch the gang's hoof-markings in the rock-hard desert floor. But there they were, climbing up into the hills.

Hardmun mounted again and followed.

His canteen was almost empty. A decision had to be made and he was loath to do it. He needed water, and he needed it now. More important, though, the mare needed it.

The heat had become oppressive as the sun reached its zenith. He had thought little about the discomfort – the stinging sweat in his eyes, the shortness of breath, the dryness of a dust-filled mouth – because the hunt had filled his mind. Now, he had lost his quarry and might well lose his life if he didn't soon find water.

For an hour Hardmun followed the hoofprints on the ground while keeping an eye out for signs of water. On these dry hills water would only collect where there were places to catch it, and shade to cool it. *Tinajas* were natural formations, some of them large bowls of rock given shape over the millennia. Rainwater was all that might fill these bowls, for streams and rivers were but a memory in this parched desert.

The mare stopped short and snorted at the air. It shook and fought Hardmun's gentle tug of the reins. Having picked up some scent, it did not want to follow the hoofprints any longer. Reluctantly, Hardmun gave the mare the reins, letting the animal pick her own trail. If it had found water, Turk would have to wait.

Dragging heavy legs, the mare climbed higher into the rocky hills. Hardmun fared little better than his mount, his strength nearly depleted. He clung to the saddle desperately, wilting over the saddle horn.

Strange, twisting spires of rock stabbed into the air along the summit above. Huge shoulders of stone poked out of the hard sand slope. The geography was promising. There might indeed be water in those rocks.

With a tired sureness, the mare made its way through the outcroppings of rock and brush and down into a partly shaded hollow. There, at the bottom of the hollow, beneath an overhanging ledge of rock, lay a shallow pool of water.

Hardmun restrained the mare for several minutes despite the powerful thirst in his own throat. He listened and watched, straining to catch sight of an ambush. He studied the ground for tracks and found none. He dismounted and climbed a stand of rounded boulders for a clearer view into the hollow. It seemed safe and empty.

Eventally he led the mare down and, after carefully sampling the water for poisonous alkali, the two drank deeply from the pool. To Hardmun, the slightly gritty water never tasted so sweet or cool.

Sated, Hardmun rinsed out his canteen and refilled it. He thought about Turk and the possibility that this *tinaja* might be the only one around for miles. Merciless nature might take Turk before a hangman's noose would have its chance for justice, or Hardmun a chance for his own.

Pebbles and dirt slipped off the overhang above Hardmun, falling on to his neck. Instantly, Hardmun dove forward into the water, turned, and wrenched his gun free of its holster. But he was too late to see anything but a flashing blade slicing down toward his throat.

Fighting down panic, Hardmun dodged the knife by rolling to his right. Doing so had pinned his gun hand, but at least he was alive. The hand holding the blade drove it deep into the muddy water even as a body slammed against him.

Hardmun rolled back against the body of his attacker, slashing with a powerful fist. He struck skin and bone and heard a yelp. The only shape he could see was a blackened silhouette in the fiery ball of the sun.

For a moment, when the pebbles had fallen onto his back, he feared he was about to be attacked by a mountain lion. He had no desire to fight such an animal, but a man was something he could handle.

Hardmun came to his feet and swung hard at the supine figure in front of him. But all he could see now was the muzzle of a big gun pointing at him.

Hardmun knocked the gun away, kicking it with his foot. A hand grabbed his leg and, pulling, knocked the heat-weakened Hardmun into the water, sending a splash of mud into his eyes.

Now it seemed as if a wild cat were attacking him. Hardmun felt the pounce of a light body and then a violent pummeling from strong arms and legs. He punched back as well, but now realized he was fighting a girl.

It took an effort to throw the girl, then to pin her beneath his strong shoulders. She snarled like a wild cat and tried to bite him.

'Enough!' he yelled, out of breath. She was tougher than she looked.

She breathed heavily for a minute then said quite calmly, 'If you let me go, I'll kill you.'

'Then I reckon I'd better keep hold of you.'

'You can't. Not all the time. You'll have to let go and then I'll kill you.'

Hardmun thought about this. 'Have you a name?'

'Ellen Vickers,' she told him, staring daggers at him. It was a disturbingly deep look. He recognized that look suddenly. This was the girl he'd seen at his hanging, the one standing on the boardwalk staring at him unwaveringly. The look she gave him sent shivers down his scarred back.

'I see,' he said.

'You bastard!' She kicked again and tried to scratch his hands.

'What now?'

'You don't recognize the name, do you?'

Hardmun thought for a moment then shook his head.

'My sister was Lucinda Vickers. Mrs Lucinda Almont.'

That name meant a great deal to Hardmun. It was the name that was to hang him. The name of the woman Turk had shot down in cold blood.

'I'm sorry about your sister. But I didn't kill her.'

'No, of course not. The law always hangs innocent men.'

Hardmun looked around and saw the girl's knife and gun. They were about twenty feet apart. He sighed. He could only retrieve one of them.

'If I let you up, will you listen to my story?'

'Go to Hades!'

Hardmun had heard tough women in his life, had listened to them swear. Never had he heard the words come out with such hatred, such damnation.

He went for the gun. Calmly, as if reaching for book on a shelf, he got up and dipped his hand toward the gun. He straightened to see Ellen was standing and holding her knife.

'Not much of a fight,' Hardmun said, gesturing with the gun.

Ellen Vickers did not answer. She charged, swinging the knife in a deadly arc. Hardmun switched the gun to his other hand, swung up with it, catching the blade with the barrel. Then he jabbed as gently he could with his fist against Ellen Vickers' jaw. She dropped heavily, and he caught her.

Hardmun helped the girl to the ground, then went to retrieve the knife. He was sliding it into his boot as the girl was getting to her feet.

'Maybe now you'll listen to me!'

Standing there proudly, slapping dust and mud from her jeans, Ellen Vickers was no girl, Hardmun noticed. She was a fireball of a woman. She had long black hair which she kept tied back with a simple string. She wore a heavy man's shirt and a well-used sombrero. There was a shape to her that the mannish clothes could not hide, and this Hardmun saw and appreciated.

'What are you doing out here?' Hardmun asked.

'I came out from St Louis to watch you die,' she said simply. 'When your gang rescued you, I set out to find you.'

'This is tough country for a woman alone.'

'I've got three canteens and food for a week. What have you got?'

Hardmun shrugged. He had a stolen horse, one canteen, and a soiled handkerchief full of linty jerked beef.

'You may remember,' he said with a wry smile, 'I had little time to prepare.'

Looking around, Hardmun could see no others had come with Ellen Vickers. He had feared that the posse might be with her, although he did not believe the colonel would allow a woman to ride with him.

He caught up the mare, saddled it and made ready to ride. He had wanted to give the animal more time to rest, but that was impossible now.

'Coward,' Ellen Vickers said.

'You rest here for the night, ma'am, then ride back to town. You shouldn't be out here.'

'I'll kill you, Link Hardmun.'

Hardmun tossed the knife back to Ellen Vickers.

'I did not kill your sister,' he told her. 'I'm after the man who did. I'll bring him to justice. I won't leave you to die, either. Your gun will be up ahead about a mile.' He nudged the mare forward and called back over his shoulder. 'Take my advice ma'am, go back to Arango. Go back to St Louis. This is no place for you.'

Behind him he heard the woman grab up the knife. For a fleeting moment he wondered if she were any good at knife-throwing, whether he had made a mistake. The knife did not come and when he looked back several minutes later, Ellen Vickers was gone.

Picking his way north, following the jagged crest of the hills, Hardmun tried again to pick up Turk's trail. The outlaw would be low on water as well. He would need to find a *tinaja* soon. His best chance to locate water would be to search up here in the cooler air.

Hardmun spent a hard day atop the mare. Dust caked his skin, sticking to greasy sweat. Along toward nightfall he had still not found Turk or the gang, although he had seen another watering hole. A careful study of the ground proved no one had been there in years, although the skeletal remains of a mountain lion attested to the infrequent availability of this pool.

Hardmun wanted to press on but fatigue was claiming him. He stopped for a moment then slipped from the saddle.

In that second a bullet missed his head, but only by inches.

He heard the crack of a rifle and then another. A second bullet beat a hole into the dust at his feet. Hardmun dove behind a rock ahead of the third bullet.

Luckily, he had guessed correctly. The shots were coming at him from behind and now he was protected by the rock. He had a revolver and plenty of bullets and he knew these would do little good against a rifle. He had to find a way to get closer to the shooter.

Hardmun moved to another rock, drawing fire. In the dim twilight he saw the red-orange flash from the muzzle of a rifle. The shooter was perhaps 100 yards away atop a fat, round boulder.

This was what he had hoped to avoid, an ambush. Turk surely had the advantage and was toying with him. The outlaw was a good shot. He would not have missed, even at that distance.

The others of Turk's gang would undoubtedly be stationed in strategic positions. Turk's plan was clear. He was drawing Hardmun to him. The others would fall in behind from some place of concealment and surround him. He thought of running but knew he would be cut down. No, he had to play the game and try to win using their rules.

Hardmun crawled from cover to cover, angling around several outcroppings of rock. He did not bother leaving his borrowed hat as a decoy for the sun had almost set and the trick was a poor one.

When he was certain he was out of Turk's sight, he began scaling the jagged back of the boulder. He holstered the gun for fear of dropping it. He could see little, but he could feel his way up to the top.

At the summit, his fingers torn from the climb, Hardmun drew his gun and worked his way back toward the last place he had seen the shooter. He waited several minutes in the gathering darkness, attempting to make out shapes. It was quickly apparent that the shooter had fled. Shortly, the moon would be up. Its glow was already visible above the peaks, Hardmun would soon be skylined, an easy target for the gunman.

Then a shape moved in the darkness. Hardmun saw the long neck of the rifle glide by within feet of him. The shooter, bent and wary, stalked in the darkness.

Hardmun leaped and crashed against the shooter. He

swung hard with a fist wanting the attack to be silent. He did not want to warn the others.

But the shooter screamed. A woman's scream.

Hardmun took the rifle and stepped back. The moon had come up, a bright three-quarters full. He could see Ellen Vickers sitting a little dazed on the rock, looking more dejected than before.

'You don't learn,' Hardmun said.

'I promised I'd kill you,' she mumbled, rubbing her jaw.

'You shouldn't make promises you can't keep.' Despite himself he was amused. He felt admiration for Ellen, too. She was tenacious, and as single-minded as he had become. She could take a punch, too.

Hardmun unloaded the rifle, pocketing the bullets.

'It's clear I cannot trust you, Miss Vickers. I wish I could. I wish I could prove to you my honesty. But I do not believe words would sway you. So I'll bring in the man who killed your sister and let the law sort out the details. Would that satisfy you?'

'You won't get the chance, Mr. Hardmun!'

Suddenly, Ellen turned sharply toward something nearby in the darkness. A chattering sound spilled into the night making Hardmun's blood run cold.

'Don't move, Miss Vickers!'

But it was too late. She screamed and threw herself aside, grabbing at her leg. On the ground a rattlesnake coiled itself to strike again.

CHAPTER EIGHT

DEATH STRIKES!

Link Hardmun drew and fired. The moonlight played tricks on his eyes, though. His first bullet struck the sand in front of the rattler, but his second cut the reptile in two.

In almost the same motion, he holstered his gun and swept Ellen Vickers up into his arms. She had turned white and wide-eyed. She shook violently. He carried her off the wide boulder and settled her on a flat rock where he tore the leg of her jeans to expose the puncture wounds. She seemed, even in her panic, to understand what Link Hardmun was about to do. She stiffened but did not pull away.

Hardmun took her large Bowie knife that he had sheathed in his boot and made a crosscut incision on the wound. Blood welled instantly. He put his mouth to the cut and began alternately sucking and spitting. He moved quickly, praying he would drain most of the poison. Ellen Vickers looked to be a strong woman. She might yet survive.

Several long minutes passed. Ellen Vickers sagged with

fatigue, then seemed to renew her strength as she pulled at her shirt and began tearing thin strips from it. Hardmun took these and wrapped them around the wound. When he had finished, he sat there for long moments, watching her. He could barely see her features in the moonlight, but he could feel the fear radiating off of her. Yet she was calm, her breathing deep and slow. Eventually, she lay back against a rock to rest. Hardmun had done all he could. It would be up to the woman now.

Leaving her, he found her horse carefully picketed in a gully. He brought Ellen to the animal and strapped her into the saddle. Then, after catching up his mare, he led them all back to the *tinaja* he had found earlier.

Wrapping the woman in his blankets, Hardmun set about to gather firewood. What he found made a meager flame, but she would stay warm through the night. The wood burned cleanly and with little smoke. He hoped the flames would not be seen.

Through the night he watched over the woman, bathing her forehead when she sweated, wrapping her in horse blankets when she shivered from the fever chill. She buried herself into his shoulder, shaking and mumbling incoherently. She did not know him, or herself, for she was only a raw nerve and no longer human.

In the quiet moments, he would drip water gently into her mouth. When she slept, he got up off the hard ground and patrolled the area around the *tinaja*. He was fearful that Turk would find him and attack. To move the woman now would mean her death and Hardmun felt he had enough blood on his hands already.

As morning neared and the sky turned a pale blue, Ellen Vickers woke with a start. She tried to sit up and found she was too weak.

'Relax,' Hardmun said. 'You do not look as if you are up to much activity yet.'

He had opened her saddlebags and found coffee, hard bread, and meat wrapped in oiled paper. These he set out in front of Ellen Vickers. He had found a small pot and a cup and began boiling coffee on the meager fire.

'You always steal a woman's food,' she said hoarsely. Her face was drained white, her eyes black. Her hair was matted and brittle. She no longer looked like a firebrand, although Hardmun still found her appealing.

'That's for you. I have my own breakfast.'

He sat down with a chunk of the jerked beef he had found in the stolen saddle-bags.

The coffee boiled. Hardmun had thrown a few mesquite beans into the pot for flavor. It was a flavor he liked.

Ellen Vickers sat up shakily and took the cup offered. She looked at the food but had no stomach for it. Then she looked long and hard at Hardmun.

'You don't look so good yourself,' she told him.

This was no surprise to him. After what he had been through in the past couple of days he was lucky to be alive. His face felt swollen, one eye was tender. The gashes on his arms and back were partly healed, though crusted over with painful, brittle scabs. Luckily, his gunshot wound had healed in jail and there was little pain now because of it.

He had slept little the past few nights and needed rest badly.

'It has been a rough few days.'

Involuntarily he rubbed his throat. It was still tender from the hangman's noose.

The gesture seemed to harden Ellen Vickers, as if she were suddenly reminded of what Hardmun was.

'I wish the rope had done its job,' she told him.

'Might have been better if it had.'

He sat and drank water and chewed on beef.

'If you didn't kill my sister, why were you charged with it.'

It was a long story, one Hardmun did not care to tell. It reminded him of all the bad things he had done in his life and of how he could never make them right again. Ellen Vickers stared with quiet, probing eyes until Hardmun felt he had to say something. Perhaps, he thought, if she knew the truth, she would return to Arango and let him finish his work.

He told her of Turk and the gang, of their flight from the country, of the ambush set by the wily colonel, and of Turk's panic to escape. Hardmun could see in her eyes an understanding growing. She sensed the tragedy about to happen again to her dead sister and shuddered. Hardmun thought to pause in the telling of the story, but the woman deserved to hear it all.

She cried silently, without sobs, then she stopped.

Hardmun did not ask if she believed him. It mattered little, he told himself. Although, in truth, it meant a great deal to him.

'You didn't die,' she said.

'No. I have yet to figure out whether that was good luck or bad.'

She reached out and touched the scabby scrapes on his arm. His sleeves were torn, as were his pant legs. Weakly she pushed and he allowed himself to be turned. The back of his shirt was shredded, too, and there were more terrible injuries on his back.

'Did they do that to you in jail?'

Hardmun smiled sourly. 'My gang did this to me.'

'But why?'

'Turk figured I talked to Sheriff Capstin or the colonel, told them how to find the rest of the gang.'

'So they rescued you just to torture you?'

'No, that was their excuse. Turk hates me. He wanted me dead, but didn't want anyone else to do it.'

Ellen shook her head in disbelief. 'Why did he think he could ride into Arango and rescue you when a posse was still after him.'

'You don't know Turk.' Hardmun laughed. 'What he lacks in brains he more than makes up for in brass.' He reddened suddenly. 'Sorry, miss, I meant to say gumption.'

A smile flickered across Ellen's face.

'The thing is, Turk is a mad dog,' he continued. 'I've got to kill him, or bring him in. Doesn't matter what happens to me. He's killed a lot of his own men, or gotten them killed. And he's done in more innocents than I care to think about. I've got to stop him.'

Neither spoke for a long time. Then he asked, 'Are you feeling stronger?'

She shook only occasionally now, when brief fever chills overtook her. Some color had come back into her cheeks. She played with her hair, concerned with the way it looked, and Hardmun took that for a good sign.

'I'll live.'

'Yes.'

The heat had grown considerably since sunrise. Hardmun put out the fire to conserve the remaining firewood. Later he would venture further out and get more. There was little wood to be found up in these rocky hills and the job would take him many hours. Hours he would lose in search for Turk. Where the outlaw had gone was a mystery to Hardmun. He prayed he would soon be able to pick up the trail again.

'You saved my life.'

He looked at her and said nothing.

'I don't know what to make of you,' she said, looking down at the ground. 'I hate you for what you are, for what they say you did. But could you have saved my life and yet have taken my sister's.'

Hardmun shook his head. 'I do not have the words to make you believe me. You have to decide that for yourself. Regardless, I will find the man who killed your sister and bring him to justice.'

'That job has been done, son,' a soft voice said behind Hardmun.

His hand flinched toward his gun butt, then stopped. It was useless, he knew. He was covered.

Hardmun turned to face the colonel. The old man stood on a rock, holding an old Sharps .54. There was enough lead in that rifle to kill three men.

'The law has seen to your trial and would have seen to your hanging if your gang had not come to your rescue.'

Hardmun snorted out a laugh. 'My rescue,' he said. He turned to reveal his torn back. 'Does this look like a rescue?'

The colonel's eyes shifted, giving Hardmun a careful inspection. He saw the wounds and the darkened eye, the torn and bloody clothing. He had seen Hardmun before the rescue and knew the man had not been so abused. The colonel's face, though, showed no emotion and barely registered the conclusion of his scrutiny.

'I don't believe he killed my sister, sir,' Ellen Vickers said from her blankets. 'But I believe he's after those who did.'

The colonel stepped down from the rock and motioned with his rifle. Hardmun unhitched his belt buckle and threw his guns where indicated by the old gentleman, toward Ellen Vickers. Then Hardmun slowly sidestepped toward a large boulder where the colonel had a clear view of him. Hardmun glanced around. There was nowhere for him to go, no cover at all.

'There are two dead men back in Arango, ma'am, dead trying to stop a jail break. He is not responsible for those deaths either, I suppose.'

Ellen Vickers was silent, deep concern etched on her face.

'The men I rode with are in these hills, mister,' Hardmun said. 'There is one among them who killed that woman. If you take me back, they'll get away.'

For a long time the nameless colonel seemed to weigh this. He knew an honest man when he saw one and he believed Hardmun to be honest. Yet he also believed in the law, and that blindfolded system had found Hardmun guilty of murder. The conflict worked within him, although it did not show on his genteel face.

'I've never heard your name,' Hardmun said, relaxing a bit against the rock. He had no plan in mind and this frustrated him.

The colonel only smiled.

'I've thought of you as a colonel and have taken to calling you that in my mind.'

His eyes narrowing slightly with amusement, the colonel asked:

'Blue or Gray?'

Hardmun said proudly, 'Gray, sir.'

'You are closer to the truth than you know, son.'

'Well, then, Colonel, I'll not attempt to trade on Southern loyalties or the name of my father's old regiment to get your sympathies. But you are a judge of men, sir. I'll trust you to judge me correctly.'

The colonel thought for a long time, a heavy irresolution knitting his brow. Getting wobbly to her feet, Ellen Vickers came to stand beside the colonel. Her concern was apparent.

'I'm sorry, son. I would like to believe you. But I have a duty.'

Hardmun slumped. 'I wish I understood that duty, Colonel.'

'We've wasted enough time,' Ellen Vickers said, bringing Hardmun's Colt up to the colonel's head. 'My sister's been killed and no man will stand between me and vengeance!'

Feeling the cold steel against his temple, the colonel did not move. His eyes shifted slightly, but his body remained rigid. Then he looked over at Hardmun.

'Forty-five, is it?' he asked with a casual air.

Hardmun nodded. He fought hard to keep down a smirk.

'My dear,' the colonel said softly, 'we are at an impasse, don't you think?' The colonel's finger was plainly and squarely on the trigger of his big rifle.

'Do you?' she asked. 'Does your duty include gunning Hardmun down, or simply bringing him back to the hangman's noose?'

Watching the colonel and waiting for a response, Hardmun rubbed his neck. The mention of the noose brought back terrifying memories, only a couple days old. He knew that those memories, so strong now, might fade in days to come, although he doubted it.

'You'll have to kill me, girl.'

'I don't think so. But if I do, so be it. I want the man who killed my sister. Hardmun can lead me to him.'

They stood very still, the three of them, each with their own private thoughts. Hardmun would not have enjoyed playing poker with either of them, least of all Ellen Vickers.

Hardmun shrugged. 'I'll bring in the real killer, colonel, and let the law take it from there.'

Slowly, the colonel lowered his rifle. Amazement swept over Hardmun. This was not something he believed the man could do.

'He won't let us go,' Ellen Vickers said, taking the rifle and dragging it to Hardmun. She kept the Colt leveled at the colonel's heart. 'We'll have to tie him up.'

'He'll die out here in this heat.'

She looked back at the old man. 'No he won't. Not this one.'

They took the colonel into the shade of a tall rock and sat him down. Hardmun tied his hands and feet. The knots were well made and strong, but they would not hold the colonel for more than two hours. He refused to leave the proud man to so ignoble a death.

Hardmun then found the colonel's horse, a gray spotted gelding with black stockings, and picketed the animal nearby. Last of all, he left the Sharps rifle close at hand.

'I'll see you down the road, colonel. Perhaps by then I can prove to you my innocence.'

The colonel gestured with his tied hands. 'This goes a long way to proving your guilt.'

Hardmun nodded then turned away. The man was right, but he had no other choice. He would not hang for another man's crime.

Ellen Vickers waited with the horses.

'Go back to Arango, Miss Vickers. You are not well yet.'

'I'm responsible for you now, Mr Hardmun. If I've been lied to, I'll kill you.'

Hardmun mounted, wondering how he had reached this point in his life, how he had got so many people hating him. The road that had once been so clear and so easy had become tortuous and cloudy. He wanted an end to it.

'Besides,' she said, mounting her sorrel pony and taking the lead, 'I'm a better tracker than you.'

They left the summit of the hills and worked their way down to a rutted path on the western slope of the range. Ellen Vickers kept her bright-green eyes toward the ground while Hardmun kept a look-out for Turk. He found his gaze drifting, though, over to the woman.

She was still pale, although a touch of pink was creeping back into her face. Soon she would recover fully. This was a strong woman. Strong, sure, and proud. Hardmun had never met a woman such as this. In his travels the women he met had only money on their minds, and used the easiest means of obtaining it. That kind had no attraction for Hardman, but he had never known any other.

'Why did you take to the owlhoot trail?' she asked casually.

'Where did you get that name?' Hardmun countered with a chuckle.

'What? Owlhoot trail?'

'Yeah.'

'Oh, well, Mr Beadles' magazines call it that.'

Hardmun laughed. 'Well, Mr Beadle has a way with fancy words, miss.'

'And you have a fancy way of avoiding a question.'

'Well, I guess I became a hold-up man because I needed money and it was the easiest way I could think of to get it.'

'You could work for it.'

'What a fella earns working is precious little, I'm told.'

'Perhaps, but it's all yours. And you've nothing to apologize for by claiming it.' When he did not offer argument, she said softly, 'It's a good life, Mr Hardmun. Difficult, but good.'

They roamed the rocky hills for several long hours. Ellen Vickers kept her eyes on the ground in a studious fashion, studying each turned or scraped stone. She was an intent woman.

Hardmun followed, for there was no better path he could have taken. He sniffed at the air and gazed in every direction. Nothing but dust and rock filled his eyes. Below them stretched a wide, dusty valley cut by the blackened, rolling lava flow.

They stopped to rest the horses and to eat. Hardmun's mare had not picked up the scent of water again.

Later that afternoon Ellen Vickers spotted a hoofprint. Hardmun examined it but could not tell if it belonged to anyone in the gang. It was fairly fresh so they followed it up to the summit of the range and down the other side. Another valley lay below them, dotted with sagebrush and clumps of grass.

There the hoofprint met up with two other sets of hoofprints and Hardmun knew these could only belong to Turk and the remnants of his gang. They had found water, of that Hardmun was certain. They could not have come so far without it.

Hardmun and Ellen Vickers continued down the hill until darkness fell.

Intending to build a fire, Hardmun began gathering bits of splintered wood. Ellen Vickers stopped him. She insisted on a cold camp. Of course she was right, but Hardmun had been thinking of her health.

He lay awake for a long time in his blankets. He

watched stars, clear and bright in black sky. When the moon came up it cast a pale yellow-white light over them. Hardmun could make out the form of Ellen Vickers in her bedroll. She lay awake as well.

'How does a girl from St Louis learn tracking like that?' he asked, his voice cracking from hours of disuse.

'I haven't spent my entire life in cities. I was born in the Dakotas, raised on a ranch.'

'What made you leave?'

She was silent for a long time. Hardmun could not make out the expression on her face.

'What is it makes a girl leave home for the big city?'

Hardmun thought for a moment. 'You are married, then.'

'No. He followed the riverboats down the Mississippi and was shot in a card game two years ago.'

Hardmun did not know what to say, so he said nothing.

'I stayed on in St Louis, though. It's a fine town. Good people.'

'I've never been there.'

The night sounds rose up in their silence. The desert was a living place, Hardmun knew, but mostly at night. Constantly he was amazed the sound the desert would make after nightfall.

'After you've caught Turk,' Ellen Vickers said, 'where will you go? What will you do?'

'You mean if they don't hang me along with him?'

The sound of a smile was in her voice when she said, 'Yes.'

'You seem sure I will get him.'

'I am.'

Her confidence in him sparked a pride he could not ever remember feeling.

'Well, I have heard there is opportunity in California. I might go there. Start a farm or a small ranch. It would not be big. I have only little money that is my own. Money I earned as a blacksmith.'

This impressed her. 'It doesn't have to be big, Link,' she told him. He could feel her gentle smile even in the darkness. Some time later they both drifted off to sleep.

The trail died at the foot of a flat, gray monadnock the next morning. No hoofprint marred the great slanted stone slope except for the occasional animal impression made millions of years ago, now frozen in time.

They paused, gazing around them. The monadnock went on for hundreds of yards and finally butted against a sheer cliff. They knew Turk could not have gone in that direction so they decided to skirt the stone slope. Hours passed and they cut no sign and saw no life.

Heat blistered the ground and made waves on the horizon. Twice they stopped to water their horses. Hardmun was becoming concerned. Ellen Vickers' strength began to wane. They would need water in another day, or sooner if the woman had a relapse. There was also the threat of Indians to consider. True, many tribes were being relocated to reservations, and the Army seemed to have a handle on the rest. But the Indian could not be discounted. Tribes still roamed free and killed with impunity.

Now, for the first time, Link Hardmun began to question this vengeance trail he traveled. The road he was on was indeed difficult. So much easier it would be to turn and run. He had enough money hidden to live well in Mexico.

Looking at Ellen Vickers, remembering the confident

sound of her voice the night before, killed all thoughts of flight in him. She had a power, Hardmun recognized. And it gave him strength as well. He would stay with this woman.

Three hours later they reached the end of the great stone slope. It seemed to slide down into the hard sand like some burrowing serpent. There were no hoofprints to be seen, but that meant little. Turk and his gang might have come out further up the monadnock.

They searched for another hour before they found the tracks. Hardmun leaped off the mare and examined the faint markings in the hard-packed sand. Then he spent ten frantic minutes searching the ground, confirming what the tracks told him.

Only one horse had come off the stone slope. The others had disappeared. Hardmun realized that Turk knew he was being followed and had circled back. The outlaw was not running away, he was leading them into a trap.

Sweat poured down the old colonel's neck and dampened his shirt. He sat very still, very composed. He was not a man to panic.

For hours he had been twisting and working at the ropes that bound his hands. He had worked carefully so as not to cut his wrists. The smell of blood would surely attract a coyote or mountain lion. Still, his wrists were chafed raw and stung brutally with sweat.

He thought of Link Hardmun. The man was a strange one. He had done nothing to help himself at trial and was prepared to die for men for whom he obviously had little regard. That code of his was one thing, stupidity quite another in the colonel's mind. Perhaps, he wondered, it was Hardmun's way of atoning.

He never thought Link Hardmun had killed that woman. But the law said he had, so that was the end of it. The colonel had lived his entire life with the law, doing its work, wearing its star. He would not abandon it now, even though his heart told him to. He would get free of his bonds then track down Link Hardmun and bring him back to the justice decreed by law.

His horse had wandered from its picket, drifting down to the pool of water. The animal drank leisurely, unconcerned. Why had Hardmun left him the horse? And the gun? The man was surely a paradox.

Another hour of careful manipulation and the colonel freed himself. There was in him no exultation or wasteful pride. He was a man with a job to do.

He had just untied the rope from around his ankles when he heard the scrape of a spur on a rock. Quickly, he draped the ropes across his feet to make it appear as if he were bound. He moved the heavy Sharps nearer, and cleared a derringer from his waistband. His revolver lay too far away to be of use.

He had just managed to wrap his hands up loosely when a man stepped into view, gun raised.

The man did not look but a moment at the colonel. He stood perfectly still, eyes narrowed. He was a young man, the colonel noted, with skin aged in the desert sun and by the hard existence of living always on the run.

His eyes moved slowly around the tiny hollow. His glance paused on the water hole. Hungry eyes, he had, and they were filled with fear. The colonel recognized the man from a sheaf of dodgers he traveled with. This was Bern Tallock, Turk's right hand man.

Tallock sidled down to the water-hole and bent beside

it. With his free hand he scooped up a palm full of water and smelled it.

'It's good,' the colonel said.

Tallock began scooping water into his mouth, dribbling much of it on to his short, scraggy beard. He never took his black, rodent eyes off the colonel.

'Where is he, old man?' Tallock asked, as he stood and continued to dart his eyes about.

'Left me for dead,' the colonel said. 'Don't expect I'll live long in this heat.' He did not sound concerned and this attracted the Tallock's attention.

'Heat mightn't get you, old man. Just who the hell are you?'

'Names are unimportant out here, boy. But I'm a man with a job to do.'

'Not no more,' Tallock said, then turned to shout out something. The colonel stopped him with a question.

'Sure you want to do that?' He had meant only to play with the man's mind, to add to the jitters Tallock had already evidenced. But his words had greater effect.

The man whirled and leveled his gun.

'Sombitch! I knowed that voice of yers. Yer that sombitch what rousted us back in those canyons. You killed Tewey!'

The colonel fired his derringer twice as Tallock pulled at the trigger of his gun. The outlaw screamed, a sound that was cut short by his rapid death. Then he fell face down into the dust.

Kicking away the ropes, the colonel grabbed up his rifle and revolver and found cover behind a large boulder. The dead man had been about to call out to a friend, perhaps to more than one. They would come now after hearing the gun shot.

Waiting, the colonel realized how thirsty he was. The pool of water at the bottom of the *tinaja* was hardly enough for him and his horse. But it looked inviting, nonetheless. He ignored it as best he could, not wanting to leave his cover.

A long ten minutes passed before he heard the scratch of leather on rock. A boot, slipping just slightly. Now the colonel could feel eyes looking down into the hollow, waiting, wondering eyes. Sweat poured down his face from the heat and stung him. Damn! he thought. I'm too blamed old for this game.

'Bern?' came a voice almost like a child's, tentative and tinny. This was Turk.

The colonel grimaced. This man was frightened, and frightened men are often unpredictable. God, how I hate amateurs, the colonel mumbled under his breath.

'You can see his legs, friend,' the colonel called out.

A volley of gunfire smashed into the hollow, kicking up dust and shattering rock.

'Who are you!?' Turk called out.

With inordinate care, the colonel edged out into the open. He held his fire, as did Turk. The outlaw, though, did not stand up from behind his cover. He peered over the rock protecting him to see the white-haired colonel standing exposed and seemingly defenseless. For a moment Turk thought to kill the man, but he had been shocked by the colonel's bold move.

When the surprise vanished from his face, Turk said, 'Ya didn't have to kill him, old man.'

'I did or he would have killed me.'

'What you want?'

'I'm after the man who killed Mrs Lucinda Almont. I believe I'm trailing him.'

Turk paled, frozen in place. The colonel's sharp eye missed nothing.

'That'd be Link Hardmun,' Turk said through pressed lips.

'The man you rescued from the gallows.'

'I have my own brand of justice, old man. I'll bring it down on him in my own time.'

'The law prescribes for justice.'

Turk laughed heartily then turned and shot the colonel's proud horse. The animal dropped, a bullet through its strong head.

'Hoof it back to town, old man. Ya might make it. But leave the justice to me.'

The colonel watched as Turk disappeared behind the rim of the hollow. He did not fire. Others of his gang might be around and he did not want to engage in a long gun battle. His quarry was still Link Hardmun, and it was Link Hardmun he would find. There would be another day for the man called Turk.

He knelt beside the dead man and searched his clothing. He had almost a hundred dollars folding money, a torn and stained letter from someone named Amanda, and a brightly colored brooch shaped as a teardrop. The colonel had a photograph in his pocket of a man and a woman. The woman was quite beautiful and she wore a brooch the shape of a teardrop, jewelry she'd never wear again.

The colonel thought on this a long time. Doubt had been in his mind for some time now, and the colonel was a man who did not like doubt. He was doubting the law now, and the justice in hanging Link Hardmun.

CHAPTER NINE

CAPTURE!

Link Hardmun had doubts of his own. He and Ellen Vickers had lost the trail of the three outlaws. Only one set of hoofprints had come down off that stone slope, and that rider had probably circled back by now. For all he knew, they were surrounded.

'Where could they be?' Ellen Vickers asked. A very quick study, she had already reached the same conclusion Hardmun had. She did not panic, though, and she did not show fear. Here was quite a woman, Hardmun thought, as his mind bent to seeing that she survived what was to come.

Hardmun gazed across the flat land. It was a deceptive plain, not truly flat at all. There were the low rolling mounds, outcroppings of round stone, and the cracked earth was veined with arroyos. Men might be seen but if they were careful, they could get within rifle range and never be spotted. Indians could crawl even closer undetected.

'We have to get out of sight,' Hardmun said and led them to a shallow arroyo.

Down inside the narrow gully, they dismounted and lay still in the sand, watching, waiting. So much of his life had been spent like this, Hardmun suddenly realized. Waiting for the stages he held up or for posses to ride by. This was no life for a man and he vowed to change it if he could. He would need help, and perhaps such help would come from Ellen Vickers.

But what could he offer a woman like that? A city woman with education and breeding? Sure, she did well out here. She was a strong woman with a clear mind and a good heart. Manlike, she had taken to the vengeance trail with more courage than Hardmun had ever seen in a woman. What would she want with someone like Hardmun?

Sensing emotion in him, Ellen reached out and touched his arm. In her face was kindness, but even that simple gesture tore at him. He deserved no kindness from her, he thought, only her contempt for his inaction. That she no longer hated him only brought him more pain.

After an hour, Hardmun could stand no more. Concerned for the safety of the woman he started them down the arroyo. They lead their horses, bending low below the rim of the arroyo so as not to be easily seen.

'We need to gain some real cover,' he told her.

'Are we running away?' she asked, angered.

'No. But we seem to be dancing around each other now, both of us blind. At least I hope they are as blind as we are. We need to gain some advantage. They are three to our two.'

Ellen Vickers accepted this silently, pausing a moment to draw her Winchester from its saddle boot.

They reached the end of the arroyo and climbed out. Hardmun wanted to try for a group of low hills ahead of them three or four miles. But it was such a long way to go, exposed and unprotected.

Ellen Vickers found another arroyo that seemed to meander toward the distant hills. They went down into it.

They had spent so much of the day tracking, and then two hours making their way through arroyos, only occasionally looking up to get their bearings. The sun was beginning to set and it made a distant red fireball on the horizon.

The blood-red mare snorted suddenly, pulled back slightly on it's reins. Hardmun did not fight with the animal. He recognized the sign. Someone was near.

He pushed their horses away and drew his gun. Ellen Vickers saw this and checked the Winchester in her hands.

The only warning Hardmun had was the falling of a pebble. He looked up and saw a man, black inside the ball of the setting sun, leaping down into the arroyo.

Hardmun could not swing his gun hand up in time to fire.

The man struck Hardmun across the top of the head with the barrel of his gun. Hardmun fell to his knees, pain rippling down his spine. The man closed in and kicked Hardmun in the stomach. He dropped to the sandy floor and curled up to protect against further blows. But none came.

He heard a scream – Ellen's – and then a shot. Sand exploded by his face.

'You yellow cur!' Ellen Vickers yelled.

Hardmun turned over and saw the man struggling with Ellen Vickers. They each held the rifle, pushing and pulling. Ellen Vickers had no chance of beating the man.

Though soft and beefy, he was tall and outweighed the woman by fifty pounds. Hardmun recognized him as one of the gang, Andy Briar.

Ellen Vickers abandoned the weapon and began hitting Briar. They were powerful blows, but not strong enough to damage the man.

Hardmun had crawled to his feet, stabbing pain cutting through his chest and stomach. He took a step forward but saw he was too late. Briar had Ellen Vickers wrapped up in his arms and was holding a gun to her head.

'Hello, Link,' Briar said, grinning stupidly. He was a strong man, Briar, and he loved to inflict pain. He twitched now with the arm that held Ellen Vickers, squeezing her throat, and Hardmun saw the woman wince.

'Hello, Andy,' Hardmun said, holding his gut.

'Mighty fine filly ya got here, Link. Didn't know ya was so handy with real women.'

Hardmun said nothing. He held Briar under piercing scrutiny. The man had a shield, holding Ellen Vickers in front of him like he did. But Briar was the kind of man who would gladly give up his advantage for the pleasure of killing someone.

'I'd like to kill you, Hardmun, honestly I would. But Turk, he says you belong to him. So I don't know's I can shoot you.'

'You do have a problem.'

'Ya see that, too, don't you? Well, damned if I can figure a way 'round this.'

Hardmun still held his gun. He might be able to shoot Briar, but not before Ellen Vickers' head got blown off.

Briar pulled at the woman, half dragging out of the arroyo. Hardmun watched them carefully, keeping the gun at the ready.

Briar got to his horse, half-hidden behind a boulder, and climbed into the saddle, never loosening his grip. Hardmun had a clear shot at the top of the man's head but hesitated. Bringing his head up, Briar smiled cruelly. He had dared Hardmun to strike, knowing the man wouldn't. From the saddle Briar shifted the arm holding Ellen and, reaching down with his hand, grabbed a fistful of the woman's shirt and pulled her up after him.

'Turk'll let me keep this here filly, for a little while at least.'

'If you harm her in the least,' Hardmun said through clenched teeth, 'I won't kill you, Briar. But you'll wish I had.'

Ellen Vickers took a deep breath. She tried valiantly to keep down what Hardmun knew had to be a growing panic.

'Yeah, ya know'd some Indians in your time, Hardmun, I remember that. Well follow me, if'n you've a mind to. But when ya catch up to me, I'll be with Turk and Tallock. We'll kill ya, then, Hardmun. We'll all put lead into ya! I promise!'

Briar fired off his pistol three times, whooping like an Apache. Hardmun's blood-red mare, spooked by the noise, bolted, nearly running Hardmun down. By the time he got the horse calmed, Briar was a mile away.

Hardmun watched the dust trail rising into the red-orange sky of the setting sun. It looked like a flame from Hell flicking its tongue in a mocking gesture.

Standing there, outlined in the red of the sun, Hardmun realized he had no choice but to follow. There was no other thought in his mind. He could ride off, of course, and be free from everything but his own conscience. Besides, Ellen Vickers had begun to hold a large place in Hardmun's thoughts. These he could not shake from his mind, nor did he want to. He would follow Briar, see the woman freed and Turk dead, even if it meant his own life.

Quickly he tied the reins of Ellen's pony to his saddle and rode off. His mare wanted to run but Hardmun kept the animal to a quick trot. He needed time to think. A trap lay ahead, but that did not mean he had to walk into it blind.

Briar was now more than a mile ahead. That meant that Turk had not been lying in wait with the others, that he had turned back for another reason. Hardmun remembered the shots he had fired and those that Ellen Vickers had fired. If the wind was right, this clear air might have carried the sound to Turk. Had the outlaw turned back because of it? That had to be it. Turk had heard the shots and turned back to investigate.

They traveled on, returning to the rocky hills. Behind Hardmun, the sun continued its slide toward the horizon. Another hour and blackness would fall. He had to end this before then.

Sensing the change of Hardmun's mood, the mare moved instantly into a strong gallop. Hardmun did not restrain the fine animal. He was racing against time now.

Briar, dragging a reluctant captive and riding double, made poor time climbing up the rocky hills. He had been laughing since leaving the arroyo with Ellen Vickers. But he no longer laughed. He had expected to find Turk by now and the gang leader was nowhere to be seen. Also, he sensed that Hardmun was now riding hard toward him. Hardmun had always been the strongest of the gang. Briar feared him greatly. He had saved them in Mexico and had warned them about the colonel as they crossed back into the States. The man was smart in a way Briar could never be, and intelligence frightened him.

He urged his horse frantically up the treacherous, rocky slope. He needed distance now, and a place to hide. Barring that, he needed a place from which to spring a trap.

Ellen Vickers said nothing, although she keenly observed every emotion etched in Briar's face. She sat awkwardly in his saddle, pressed up to the horn, her added weight slowing them down. Briar had paused earlier to bind her to the saddle horn. It was a poor, hasty effort and she found the knots loosening.

She vowed not to make her escape. Though frightened, she knew Briar could lead her to Turk, the man who killed her sister. She wanted more than anything in life to come face to face with Turk.

Hardmun's mare took to the rocky slope like a mountain goat. Sure-footed and fast, the animal gained rapidly on Briar, Ellen's riderless pony keeping pace. Ahead, he could see Briar whipping at his horse, urging it on with hoarse, anxious curses. Soon the man would have to turn and fight.

Hardmun did not give him the chance. He turned out toward a clump of rocks and, using them for cover, climbed above Briar. There he dismounted and sent the horses away. With revolver drawn and Winchester in his left hand, he worked his way back toward the path Briar had taken.

He crested a small rise but only saw a dust trail settling below him. Briar had turned off as well. Hardmun could see the trail vanish between two large boulders.

He slid down from the short rise and crossed to the boulders. He climbed one of the rocks, unwilling to enter the narrow pass between them. This was certain to be a trap, to Briar's less than clever mind.

Peering over the rim of the boulder, lying flat on his stomach, Hardmun saw what he expected. Briar waited, crouched behind a rock, rifle cocked and ready. He did not see Ellen Vickers immediately. Then he spotted her shoulder behind another rock. She had been tossed there, that was clear. But he did not know if she was alive or dead.

Briar waited directly below Hardmun, a little more than twenty feet. Hardmun took its measure then set the rifle down and holstered his gun. Very calmly he edged up to the rim and calmly stepped off into space.

He hit Briar squarely on the shoulders, driving the man into the dust. He rolled away after impact, slightly disoriented, a cloud of dust curtailing his vision. Briar screamed and cursed. He had dropped his gun and, as if blinded, searched the ground for it.

On his feet, Hardmun swung a heavy fist down on Briar's head. The man screamed again and pulled away, his eyes glazing.

Panic drove Briar away. He crawled on his back, feet and hands kicking.

'Take her, Hardmun. Ferget it! I didn't mean nothin'!'

'If you've harmed her, Briar,' Hardmun said, a menacing silhouette in the gray twilight, 'I'll kill you.'

'Naw, she's OK! I swear!'

Briar continued to back away even though Hardmun had not advanced. He looked around in rabbit-like glances, his face terrified beyond reason. Then, almost too late, Hardmun saw why. Briar had spotted his fallen gun and was making for it, feigning terror.

Briar lunged to his right, his hand falling easily onto his gunbutt. He rolled completely over and came up firing.

His shot rang out a split second too late. Hardmun had already drawn and fired his own gun, catching Briar in the throat.

Shock filled Briar's eyes as death came to him quickly. He groped at his chest trying desperately to claw the bullet out of him. A moment later he was dead and he fell face down on to a rock.

Approaching hoofbeats echoed suddenly in the narrow draw. Hardmun whirled and fired in the same instant. This time, his shot came too late as a body flew into him, knocking him onto his back. A fist slammed into Hardmun's face and he felt blood trickling from his mouth.

Turk!

The outlaw scrambled to his feet, laughing and loosely holding a gun in his hand. A trickle of blood escaped his lip and he wiped it away with a rough gesture. Breathless, he laughed again.

'Glad ya killed him, Hardie,' he said, looking down at Briar. 'Boy was jest too crazy for my likin'.'

Hardmun pulled himself to his knees. He checked for his gun and found it gone. Turk made a noise and when Hardmun looked up he saw Turk holding the gun in front of him, tauntingly. He twirled it in his hand a few times so Hardmun couldn't mistake it then tossed it across the draw.

'Ya come a long way to die in a hole like this, Hardie. Maybe we shoulda let thet hangman do his duty.'

'Maybe,' Hardmun said sourly.

There was a murmur from behind a rock and then Ellen Vickers got shakily to her feet. She untied her loose bonds and looked around as if through a haze. Her pants were torn at the knee and her shirt was torn, too. There was a bloody scrape at her elbow and her hair and clothes were in disarray. But otherwise she appeared all right. A wave of relief washed over Hardmun.

'Well!' Turk said. 'Very fine indeed.' Turk shifted so he could keep both Ellen and Hardmun in view. But they were too far apart to be covered by one gun.

'And just who are ya, lady?' Turk asked, full of smugness.

'I'm Ellen Vickers. You killed my sister.'

'Damn!' Turk spat. 'How long I gotta be hounded for that?' Turk did not allow time for an answer. In one swift motion he leveled his gun and shot Ellen Vickers.

'You bastard!' Hardmun screamed, throwing himself at the outlaw.

With one leap he rammed the big man, pinning his gunhand. Hardmun grabbed the revolver, pushing it toward Turk's stomach. They struggled mightily, knocking each other with their free hands.

Eventually the gun twisted out of Turk's hands and fell to the ground. Hardmun kicked it away savagely. He wanted no weapon. He wanted to tear Turk apart using only his bare hands.

He swung down hard with his right, catching Turk behind the ear. Blood spurted from a gash in Turk's head. Then he swung up with his left and flattened Turk's nose.

But the outlaw was big and tough and could take much punishment. He slammed into Hardmun with his shoulder, shoving him up against the boulder. Hardmun gasped, his lungs emptied by the force of the blow. He felt one fist then the other hit him across the face.

Dropping beneath the blows, Hardmun had a split second with which to regain his breath. Fighting panic, he drew in a heavy, wheezing breath.

Now he threw a powerful right jab into Turk's crotch. The outlaw crumbled to his knees, groaning animal sounds. Hardmun backhanded Turk, then set into him with a series of lefts and rights. A long minute of this punishment passed and still Turk did not fall over. Finally, nearly spent himself, Hardmun found strength for one last blow that toppled the indomitable Turk.

Hardmun retrieved his gun. He sat down heavily in the dust, nightfall closing in. He could just make out Turk's prone form. He lay there groaning, wanting to push himself off the ground but with no strength to do so. The man had lost. He had no will to continue the fight.

The sound of a hammer cocking awakened Hardmun from his stupor. Ellen Vickers was alive. Hardmun could see a cut on her forehead and a bloody slash in the arm of her shirt above her bloodstained elbow.

She stood over Turk, a pistol cocked and pointed at the man's head. The look of determination she wore frightened the outlaw. He saw in her eyes, glinting in the last light of the day, his own death.

Ellen Vickers meant to kill Turk. He had killed her sister, had taken a good and sweet life and snuffed it out without a thought. Her own life would have ended the same way, with a bullet fired from Amos Turk's gun, if Providence had not intervened. Somehow she was meant to live, meant to deliver justice to her sister's killer.

But then what of Link Hardmun, she thought. How would his name ever be cleared? Ellen Vickers stood for a long time, unmoving, thinking.

The powerful rush of relief he had felt in seeing her alive had given way to concern for her. He could see her determination, read her thoughts. She was about to step into a terrible world.

'Are you sure this is what you want to do?' Hardmun asked, standing beside her. He would not stop her killing Turk if that were what she wanted, though he prayed she would not commit murder. She did not look up at him. Could not. Not yet.

'I don't know. I want to kill him. I hear my sister crying out and I see his ugly face standing over her laughing. I could kill him. But is she crying out for vengeance, or to stop me from doing something horrible?'

'I ain't spent much time in church to know the difference.'

She closed her eyes briefly. 'I have, and I should know the difference. If I kill him, you'll never be free. My word about what Turk did won't be enough to keep the law off of you. You'd be hounded the rest of your life for something he did.'

'Bringing him back to face trial won't be enough, Ellen. He's slick. He could get away with the murder.'

'It might be enough, if I go back and tell them what I know.'

'We'll both go back,' he said.

She looked up now, barely seeing him in the dark. She knew the bruises he carried on his face and these she touched gently. The moon was coming up, and it was nearly full. She'd be able to see him better soon.

'No. I'll take Turk back and I'll see him hung, legally. The colonel knows enough about him to get that job done. But you can't come with me.'

'I'll be free, Ellen,' he told her.

'Will you? You're still a fugitive. And do you think the colonel will let you go again?'

She was right, of course. But Hardmun did not wish to ask someone to do what was his job to finish.

'You said you wanted to go to California. Go, then. You'll be safe there. You can start a new life.'

Hardmun pressed closer to Ellen Vickers. 'I want a new life, Ellen. But not alone. I know that now.'

The newly risen moon cast a pale glow into the draw and Hardmun could see her smile.

'You'll not be alone, Link. I promise you that.'

He drew the woman to him, scooping her up in his arms, and bent his head toward hers. He kissed her. Softly at first and then hard and longingly. After a while, she pushed herself away by touching his chest gently.

'I'll go with you as far as town,' he told her. 'The colonel won't expect that. By the time he gets back to Arango our business will be done.'

He could see by her face that she didn't like the plan. It was too dangerous for him. But now that she had declared herself to him she never wanted to leave his side.

'OK,' she sighed. 'But if he tries anything, I'm the one who gets to shoot him.'

Turk groaned as Hardmun hauled him to his feet.

'I'll see you hanged, too, Hardie boy,' he taunted through cracked lips.

Hardmun looped a rope around the big man's wrists then yanked tight the knot he had tied. Turk winced and grunted.

'Have your fun,' Turk whispered.

'You're a murderer, Turk. It's time you paid for your crimes.'

Turk laughed, throwing back his head. The move was so sudden and loud that Ellen cocked the gun in her hand and stuck the barrel into the outlaw's beefy side.

'No need for that, little lady. Aw, Hardie, you fool. You're in this as deep as me 'cause they all want to believe you're a killer.' He laughed again, although not as loud. 'How many times did you stop me from killing, Hardie?'

'Not enough,' he said bitterly.

'That's right. They want you to be a murderer, so you are.'

Hardmun shook his head. 'No. I'm better than that. At least now I am. I feel like I've woken up, Turk, like a horrible dream has ended and I'm awake enough now to live.'

'Until they hang you, boy. Until they hang you.'

With a shove, Hardmun sent Turk stumbling toward a large rock. He told the outlaw to sit down then tied his legs together.

'We'll camp here for the night. In the morning we head back to Arango.'

Ellen was by his side now, a soft hand on his arm. He couldn't see her face clearly and desperately wanted to. He might have very little time left in this world and he wanted to spend every minute of it drinking in her eyes.

'This isn't just about returning Turk, Link,' she said. 'I don't have to see your face to know that.'

He turned and said, 'I'll see if I can scrounge up some firewood.' She didn't release his arm. He didn't want to pull free from her, but he didn't want to tell her the truth, either.

'That sheriff,' she said. 'You're going back for him, aren't you.'

For a long moment he didn't say anything. 'He's holding that town hostage, Ellen. He terrorizes them, beats them, and steals from them. He's got to go.'

'Link, I know he hurt you in that jail cell, but don't go back seeking revenge. That would make you a killer.'

'I'll give him a chance to go easy.'

'He's the law in that town. If you kill him you'll have

every lawman on you no matter where you go. And I won't be with you, Link. I want to be with you, but I won't. Not if you do this.'

Hardmun stiffened, his shoulders squaring.

'I know. But I can't leave that town to him any more. I did that once. I saw what he was and what he had done, and I still left. I should have killed him then.'

'So you'll kill him now?'

'It doesn't have to be that way. I'll take the gun from his hand and lock him up. The people will turn on him, then.'

'Are you so sure, Link? Do you really believe they will?'

He said nothing because he didn't know what to say. He had no answers. Cowed as those townspeople were, they might be too afraid to save themselves. But the image of that saloon girl was in his mind, the trickle of blood on her mouth, the milky glaze in her dead eyes. The image brought another to mind. A horror he had witnessed as a boy. He should never have let himself be chased off. He should have finished the job.

The fire he built was small and cast little heat or light. They bedded down near it, Hardmun sitting further away from the flames facing Turk. He dozed a little during the night and in the morning was exhausted. His face was stiff and throbbing and he could feel several lumps on his forehead and on the back of his head. Wearily he got to his feet and kicked the fire out.

'What? No coffee?' Turk asked with a lopsided smile. His face was bruised as well, but he wore the damage like a second skin, as if this was his natural appearance. The fear he had felt the night before was gone. It was a long ride back to Arango, and the outlaw felt that anything could happen along the way.

'Get up. We've a long ride.'

With Turk in the lead, they headed south along the cracked and brittle earth. Their passing kicked up a column of dust and, occasionally glancing along their backtrail, Hardmun watched it rise high into the air. Not long after sunrise the air became stifling and oppressive with heat. They rested in the shade of an arroyo and watered the horses using their hats as troughs. Much of the day they walked rather than rode to conserve the horses' strength.

So much had happened since his hanging that he had lost track of time. Had he been out here two days, or three? Or was it more?

By late afternoon Hardmun's mare snorted and lifted its head. It began pulling at the reins, trying to angle off toward a saddleback ridge. There was shade under the ridge so Hardmun let the horse lead the way. The others followed limply.

As they neared, all of the horses lifted their noses and, finding new energy, began walking briskly toward a cut in the hill. The hill was a shallow slope of rock and dirt and the occasional scrub brush. There were several green bushes clumped together just under the rim of the hill on a narrow ledge at the back of the cut. Below the bushes was a small pool of water.

Hardmun let the horses drink first, pulling them back before getting their bellies too full. Ellen drank next and then refilled her canteens. There was enough left for each of the men to quench their thirst, but not much more. A soft trickle of water dribbled out of the rock into the drained pool.

'By morning it should be refilled,' Hardmun said.

After seeing to the horses, he went back to check on the

pool. It was filling quickly.

Ellen had collected a pile of twigs and brush and was slapping two pieces of flint together to start a fire. Hardmun stopped her.

'We're heading back into whatever posse might be left. I'd like not to let them know where we are.'

'You said that only the colonel remained.'

'Probably. But let's not risk being seen anyway.'

Her face hardened for a moment then a soft light came into her eyes. 'Do you really want to kill him that bad, Link?'

'I won't kill the colonel, Ellen. Even if he drew on me. I don't think I could it.'

'I meant Capstin.'

'Oh,' he said, then went to their bedrolls without answering her. Again he tied Turk's legs and sat him down next to a rock. Hardmun took his bedroll to the mouth of the cut.

'It'll be cold,' she told him. 'Without a fire.'

'We'll be all right.'

Their meal of jerked beef and water left each dissatisfied. The sun set with a bloody beauty, cut briefly by the blue scratch of a high, thin cloud. Hardmun watched for a long moment before turning his attention back to Turk. The outlaw sat calmly, grinning, eyes locked on Hardmun. Turk had a plan; Hardmun could see that clearly in the outlaw's menacing stare. Whether it was to escape or to kill Hardmun, or both, he didn't know. And he didn't know when that plan would be sprung. All of the gang were dead, so Turk could expect no help from them. Or were they?

'You get some sleep, hear?' Turk said. 'Just rest your poor, tired eyes.' Hardmun did not answer. 'You gotta rest some time. . . .' Turk's words trailed off as he spotted something off in the distance.

Turning, Hardmun saw it, too. Far off in the distance at the base of the hill a camp-fire glowed. Ellen came forward and placed a hand on his arm.

'Who is it?'

Hardmun shook his head. It couldn't be anyone trailing them on their return to Arango, or so he believed. Someone trailing them wouldn't risk a fire. Ellen, Turk, and Hardmun had started the day walking on rock, then, after that, dry, hard-packed earth. They would not have left much of a trail to follow, and few men would be able to read the faint sign. The colonel would, though. He had dogged Hardmun's trail for so long it was as if the man could read his thoughts. As if he knew where Hardmun would go before he did.

If it was the colonel then he had lost their trail come nightfall. Only black-hearted coincidence had put him so close. The man would have no idea they were near.

'In the desert air my voice'll carry,' Turk whispered. 'All I have to do is call out and he'll know where you are.'

A chill ran through Hardmun. This outlaw before him he could kill, would kill gladly. But the colonel . . .

'I'll kill you if you do,' Hardmun said, lifting his gun.

'He'll hear that, too.'

Getting to his feet Hardmun went over to Turk, turning his gun in his hand. The outlaw saw the motion and his eyes shot wide looking at the heavy gunbutt held like a hammer.

'I don't take pain well, Hardie. I'll scream, I promise.'

'Link?' Ellen said.

He ignored her. Grabbing Turk by his greasy hair, Hardmun yanked the outlaw's head back and shoved him to the ground. Turk's mouth opened in shock and at that moment Hardmun jammed the gunbutt into his mouth. From his boot Hardmun took the long knife he had removed from Turk earlier and placed the blade against the man's throat.

'You won't make a sound,' Hardmun said. 'Not a single word.'

'Link, please,' Ellen whispered.

A smile came into Turk's eyes, cruel and black. If Turk was anything, it was a shrewd judge of men. He knew instinctively how far he could push a man, how much he could get out of one before the man collapsed or had to be killed. Turk knew he had not yet pushed Hardmun to his breaking point.

With the gun removed, Turk laughed softly.

'I could cry out, Hardie, even before you sliced me with that pig sticker. Bring the law down on us. He'd kill you dead.'

'You want me dead so bad then why didn't you let Capstin finish me?'

'Capstin was a scared fool, rushing you to a fixed trial, hurrying the hanging.'

'What did he have to be scared of?'

Turk grinned. Hardmun felt a sick churning in his stomach looking at the man's confidence. Tied, held at gunpoint, Turk knew something that emboldened him.

'You and Capstin have been working together,' Hardmun said, sure in his sudden realization.

'He has his uses.' Turk shifted and leaned against the rock with his right shoulder. 'He figured you would talk, that you knew about his connection to me.'

'I didn't.'

'He didn't know that. He needed you shut up fast.'

'Then why not let him finish me?'

'Because I hate you, Hardie,' Turk spat. 'Through and through. Hated you from the first, but you were useful. Hate that fat slob of a sheriff, too, and he ain't so useful no more. No, Hardie, I want to go back, 'cause you and me are going to wreak a little vengeance. And then I'm going to kill you.'

CHAPTER TEN

BACK TO ARANGO

Hardmun slept little that night. He watched the distant camp-fire, barely more than a tiny flicker nestled within a black backdrop, trying to discern movement. In his mind he imagined the colonel using the fire to distract attention as he slipped over the hill toward the shallow cut in which the fugitives were hidden. The littlest sounds made him jump. Behind him Turk slept peacefully, a crooked grin on his face.

Twice Hardmun left his post to walk around their camp, to stretch his legs, he told himself. But the truth of it was he was afraid of being caught by surprise. He went up the hill a ways, moving with great care, willing his boots to be silent. His heart jumped when he heard pebbles tumbling downhill, and only calmed when he realized his own feet had kicked loose the stones. After that he meekly returned to his bedroll. Ellen had not woken with his movements and a narrow-eyed glance over at Turk showed the outlaw had not moved. Still, that grin was on his face and his head now was tilted toward the left. He had seen Hardmun leave camp, and had known why. Turk was amused and that left Hardmun feeling a bit foolish.

In the morning, bleary-eyed and tired, he drank some water and chewed on some of the dried meat, never letting his gaze stray from the horizon. The camp-fire had gone out with the first hint of daylight. Try as he might, he could see nothing of the mysterious rider. Turk grumbled about the heat that would soon bake down on them, wanting to get started for Arango.

Hardmun ignored him and kept watching the horizon. After an hour he was able to spot a dust trail rising further west of where the camp-fire had been. He waited another hour to make certain the rider was moving away.

'Let's saddle up,' he said, finally.

'We'll kick up our own dust trail,' Ellen reminded.

Hardmun shook his head. 'We'll go up on the hill. It's mostly rock there. Once on the other side it won't matter. That rider will be so far out he won't see our dust.'

It took some time to saddle the horses and mount up. Turk offered no direct resistance, but with his hands tied behind his back he made for a clumsy rider. Hardmun kept close to the outlaw, twice catching him before he fell out of the saddle.

They moved slowly. The horizon offered them nothing to look at except blue waves that made an indistinct line which at times looked close enough to touch. Hardmun paused at the patch of *choya* Turk had tried to run him through. Had that only been days ago, he wondered. Looking up he found Turk grinning with remembrance. They weren't far now from town. Another day and they would reach Arango.

The heat seemed to pour down on them like a heavy, never-ending stream. An hour before sunset they found another small *tinaja*, not much more than a crack in the rock through which a trickle of water collected in a surprisingly deep but compact pool. They let the horses drink first, bringing hatfuls to them, and had to wait several hours for the pool to replenish before they drank.

Exhausted, the three dropped against a short rock wall and fell asleep. The desert cold woke Hardmun to find Turk watching him in the pale moonlight. The man was smiling evilly.

'Didn't figure you had such a decent streak, Hardie,' Turk said softly.

'It ain't about decency.'

Turk glanced past Hardmun to Ellen curled up in a ball against the rock.

'It's guilt driving you this time,' he said.

'Shut up, Turk. Save your breath for the judge.'

Shaking his head, Turk said, 'Hardie, you and I both know I ain't never gonna see no judge. I figure we're close to Arango. Tomorrow we'll be there. Tomorrow's when you'll die.'

'Maybe, but you're going with me.'

Turk grinned indulgently. Hardmun hated the man now more than ever. To be so calm and sure in the face of death. To utterly believe he would survive judgment and live to terrorize again. Hardmun wondered that a man could be so cruel.

'You got nothing to smile about, Turk,' Hardmun said, feeling his jaw tighten painfully. The outlaw was baiting him, wanting him to make a mistake. But Hardmun had resigned himself. He had to maintain calm, not because he thought he could be saved but because he owed it to Ellen and her dead sister. And that little child. He had so much to atone for. He never could, he told himself. Not in a hundred lifetimes. But he could use this one life to make a start making amends. 'Your gang is dead, and you've no friends in town.'

'Don't need friends. I got the law. And the law wants you dead.'

If Sheriff Capstin was in league with Turk, Hardmun didn't stand much of a chance. Still, it was the only chance he was willing to take.

Something must have flickered across Hardmun's face because Turk brightened with renewed malevolence.

'She doesn't know, does she?' Turk asked.

Hardmun turned to see Ellen still asleep. She was curled up trying to keep warm in the chill desert air. The saddle blanket she had used to cover herself had fallen away. Hardmun pulled it about her shoulders.

'She thinks bringing me in will end this.' Turk almost looked sorry for Ellen. 'She don't know you're gonna die so you can have a bit of redemption.'

Hardmun stood, his legs stiff and fists balled.

'Guess I know a thing or two about you, Hardie. You always was predictable. Never knew an outlaw with such a soft heart.'

Standing over the man, Hardmun swung his fist with a lightning cut across Turk's face. Turk grunted and toppled over backwards. Like a giant tortoise he struggled up off his back into a sitting position, using only his shoulders to lift himself, his hands still tied behind him. His mouth was bleeding and already beginning to swell. But he was smiling.

'You can't keep hitting me, Hardie. At some point it just ain't gonna do no good. Of course, I might not tell her. Not until it's too late, that is. Yeah,' he said, warming to the torment he was inflicting. 'That's what I'll do. Maybe.'

Hardmun, rage burning in him, watched as Turk settled back against a rock and went to sleep.

They were moving early the next morning. There wasn't much to see in this broken land that the sun baked every day. Heat built up quickly and lifted off the hard, dusty ground anemically, then hung lifeless in the stagnant air. The animals stepped heavily, even from the outset. After days of punishment they were nearly spent.

The sun had drifted past its zenith by an hour or so when the horizon cleared for a moment to reveal the outline of low wooden structures. Hardmun stopped and using his kerchief wiped his face and hair and the inside of his hat. He had one last job to do, now, and it would be all over. A deep, dull pain wrenched at his stomach and he was overcome with the desire to hold Ellen one last time. But he wouldn't even look at her – couldn't. Not if he was to finish this properly.

Filled with her own thoughts, she didn't recognize his struggle.

'Link, you stay here while I take Turk into town.'

He didn't turn toward her, and for a long moment he said nothing. She waited for him to speak, but when he didn't she gathered up her reins and made ready to ride off.

'I can't do that, Ellen,' he told her, quietly, the sudden sound of his voice like the distant crack of a rifle.

'You can't go in,' she told him. 'Not until I get Turk in a cell and find a judge.'

'You won't get ten feet, Ellen. Capstin and Turk are in league.'

She threw a hard look at Turk. 'Then you believe that killer?'

His eyes only on the horizon, he said, 'I want you to give

me a head start – about an hour – before you ride in.'

'What?'

'You can't come in with me.'

'Link, you said . . .'

'I know what I told you, Ellen.' Stealing himself, he turned his eyes toward her. She was startled by the grave look she read in them. And she was so beautiful, it was all he could do to stay in the saddle and not reach out to hold her. 'But if you try to follow me,' he warned, 'I'll shoot your horse out from under you.'

Turk, who had been watching silently, burst out with laughter.

'He is a noble one, ain't he, miss? It's about all you can do to keep from shooting him yourself!'

'An hour, Ellen. It'll all be over by then. One way or another.'

Ellen's face filled with impotent rage. 'He killed my sister.'

'He'll pay. We both will.'

Hardmun flicked the reins and his horse moved forward at a trot. Turk's horse followed, its reins tied to Hardmun's saddle. Twisting around in his saddle, Turk grinned back at Ellen. 'I'll be back for you, pretty lady. Count on it.'

For nearly two days now Hardmun had been wracking his brain for a plan. None had presented to him, other than riding up to the jail and depositing Turk. He knew the outlaw had to be brought to justice, but in his mind justice had always meant death. Ellen needed more than that. She needed to see the law work against Turk, and the only way to make that happen was to bring Turk in. Getting him into Arango was the problem. Some of the townspeople – those beholden to Capstin – might try to take on Hardmun. Still, most of them had been long since cowed by the vicious sheriff. Just the curiosity of Hardmun riding back into town might keep things from degenerating into gunplay. That, at least, was his hope.

Capstin hadn't been part of the posse. Hardmun remembered the fat man had been shot during Turk's raid. He remembered, too, the sheriff triggering the trap door himself as Hardmun had stood helpless, bound and with his head in a noose. Bile rose up in Hardmun, but he forced it down. There would be justice for Capstin, too, even if it meant Hardmun would be hung for a second time.

If Capstin lived he might be lying in bed now because of his wounds. That would leave his deputies, Bill Glasser and Arch Tobler. Neither of these men would present much of a problem. With Turk's men gone, Hardmun could see little to impede to his simple, straightforward plan. So why was there something crawling in the pit of his stomach? And why was Turk grinning as he neared his end? Was it just his own brand of madness, or did he have a plan?

Hardmun paused on the outskirts of town, not more than a hundred yards from the nearest building. With the heat of the day in full swing there were few people out on the street. The saloons would have their share of hardcases, and these might venture out to look at the new arrivals. Everyone else, though, Hardmun reasoned, would stay shut in until the air cooled after sundown.

He dismounted and untied the reins to Turk's horse, then wrapped them several times around the horn of Turk's saddle.

'I could ride better with my hands in front of me,' Turk said, grinning.

'Too good. Get ahead of me,' Hardmun said with a toss

of his head. 'But not too far, hear?'

Turk chuckled, shifting in his saddle. 'I hear you, Hardie.'

Remounted, Hardmun circled around behind Turk and slapped the animal on the rump. It started with a jolt, almost throwing Turk from the saddle, then settled into a steady walk. Hardmun followed.

Arango was as quiet as he had expected. Scanning the buildings, the rooftops, Hardmun looked for anyone who might challenge him. Their dust trail would have been visible for miles. Their arrival would not have surprised anyone.

Several men looked out from the shade of saloon doors. Other faces, barely more than wide eyes, looked out from shop windows or from behind the lacy curtains of private homes. The streets were empty of horses or wagons.

They passed the gallows in the center of town, already aging under the brutal sun. The frayed hangman's rope-end hung straight and unmoving in the still air. Hardmun found himself watching it as they passed, unable to remove his eyes from it. Then he shifted straight in his saddle again. Turk was turned, looking at him, grinning. For a moment Hardmun had to fight the urge to draw his gun and kill the man.

Further beyond was the sheriff's office. The end was near now, and that was all Hardmun could think about. The ending.

They dismounted, Turk more falling from the saddle than stepping down. But even this indignity did not wipe the smirk from the man's face. The office door was open a crack, only blackness visible beyond it.

'Up you go, Turk,' Hardmun said, motioning toward

the door. Then he froze. Something about that door made him wary. It was a trap. But was it inside? Or would they wait until he had gone into the sheriff's office before rushing it? He would have nowhere to run once inside. He'd be as trapped as Turk. Then with a shrug he again motioned for the outlaw to mount the two steps to the front door. He hadn't planned on being able to leave anyway, not alive.

Turk took the first step then the second. Suddenly, his foot slipped and he tumbled forward onto his face. Had there been a shot? Hardmun leaned forward just as the big outlaw lifted his leg and jammed it backward, catching the onrushing Hardmun in the chest. Hardmun bounced backward, landing in the dust, the wind sucked from his lungs.

Turk was on his feet now, his hands balled into huge fists held in front of him, the ropes dangling from his wrists. The man had freed himself.

Hardmun rolled to his right and came up onto one knee then hurled himself forward. He caught the outlaw with both arms, jamming his head into the man's gut. Turk let out a grunt and fell backwards, Hardmun clinging to him. Bringing one knee up in a ferocious kick, Hardmun missed his target and fell helplessly away. Something heavy slammed into his head and he dropped into the dust.

He felt Turk claw at him and in desperation swung his elbow wildly around until it cracked into something hard. Behind him Turk groaned and let go.

Spinning, Hardmun could see men coming tentatively out into the street. A shot rang out. He felt a tug at his arm, pain shooting like a hot razor along his shoulder. Dipping his right hand, he fingered for the gun at his hip, but it wasn't there. Turk had taken it from him.

The big outlaw was lying in the street, a hand to his face, blood pouring from above his eyebrows. He cursed and wiped blood from his eyes, and all the while his gun hand wavered, trying to get a bead on Hardmun. With a swipe of his foot Hardmun kicked dust into the outlaw's eyes, blinding him. Hardmun was about to throw himself onto Turk when another shot – this one from behind – ricocheted off the dirt.

Weaponless, Hardmun ran for the nearest building and ducked around the corner as two more shots chased him. Arango had only one street, with a couple of broken wide alleys that crossed it at odd angles. There was a shed behind him and a long open stretch to Gepson's livery stable where a couple of fly-tormented nags stood roasting in the afternoon sun. Hardmun ducked and ran for the dark safety of the barn.

Turk got to his feet shakily, using his sleeve to wipe away blood. A crowd had gathered round him, curious and anxious for action. Bill Glasser, with his long, stringy, yellow hair and dusty bowler hat, ran up to Turk and pointed excitedly toward where Hardmun disappeared. He fired off two quick shots that slapped harmlessly into the side of a house.

'Where's Capstin?' Turk growled.

The other deputy, Arch Tobler, his face full of red pimply blotches, came up from the other side of the street. His right wrist was still swollen from Hardmun's attack days ago and was wrapped in bandages. The deputy favored it slightly, holding it close to his body. His gun was tucked into his belt rather than his holster, ready for a left-handed draw.

'I seen him run to the livery stable,' he said excitedly.

'Capstin?'

'No, Hardmun. He's holed up in Gepson's livery. The sheriff's in his office, waiting.'

'Hey,' someone called from the crowd. 'Ain't you that outlaw that busted up the hanging?'

The others in the crowd had recognized Turk as well, and had begun moving out of the street. Turk turned and, finding the man who had spoken, lifted his gun and fired. The man dropped soundlessly, dead.

'We finish this now,' Turk said.

They found Capstin inside the sheriff's office, gun raised, waiting. Seeing Turk framed in the doorway his shoulders slackened with disappointment.

'You let him get away,' the fat sheriff accused.

Turk eased through the door and went to the large desk across the room. There was a bottle of whiskey sitting there, open, next to a glass. Turk threw a leg over the edge of the desk and set his gun down to pour himself a drink. He swallowed as if it had been years since he last drank whiskey.

'I told you I would kill him, Capstin. I didn't want him hung,' Turk said, quietly.

'It's the law, Turk. He killed a woman and her baby. Besides, I didn't want him talking.'

'I told you to let him go.'

Glasser and Tobler came to the doorway, blotting out some of the sunlight with their long shadows.

'Couldn't do that, Turk. I'm the law. Only way I keep this town is with an iron grip. I give in at all and they'll turn on me.'

'You're a dirty louse, Capstin. You ain't no law. You're only here because I want you to be. And I told you to leave Hardmun to me.'

Despite the shadows Turk could see the sheriff's large belly moving with his rapid breathing. The hand holding the revolver was shaking slightly.

'I got the gun, Turk. I'm the law. I think maybe you ought to get into that cell over there.'

To Turk's right one of the cell doors stood wide open.

'You should have listened, Capstin. I'll kill Hardmun. That's my chore.'

With a lightning sweep of his hand, Turk's gun was lifted and fired. The bullet struck Capstin in the chest before the man could react. An instant later he tumbled to the floor, dead. Tobler and Glasser seemed wedged in the doorframe, terrified, unable to move.

'You can die,' Turk told them. 'Or you can help me kill Hardmun. Which'll it be?'

The two men said nothing, only nodded dumbly.

Turk grinned and said, 'Let's go.'

There were pitchforks and shovels and a heavy wooden block and tackle rig, but no guns and no knives. The stable smelled musty and sour. The animals in the stalls fidgeted, sensing trouble. The place was dry and crackling, a tinder-box that would ignite with the least effort, and Turk was the sort who would set it ablaze just to watch it burn.

Hardmun watched out the main door at the meeting in the street. He saw Turk shoot a man in cold blood and wondered where Capstin was hiding. There had been another shot – a few minutes later – which came from the sheriff's office. And now Turk was on the street, but not Capstin. Had the sheriff been waiting in ambush for them in his office, he wondered. It would be in keeping with his cowardly style. Hardmun mentally put a check mark beside Capstin's name. There were only three of them now. But three of them with guns.

Escape through the front of the barn was blocked. There was a back door and a door that opened into the corral that was attached to the stable. Outside Hardmun could see the three gunmen approaching. With a wave of his hand, Turk motioned for Tobler to take the front and Glasser to circle around toward the corral. Turk himself disappeared behind a building down the street as he moved to his left. They approached cautiously, but quickly.

Keeping to the shadows, Hardmun ran to the stalls and cleared them of the few wiry and flatbottomed horses grazing there on stale straw. The animals moved sluggishly as he aimed them toward the corral door. Crowding through the narrow opening two of the horses bucked, but the heat had drained them of much of their energy. Surrounded by them, Hardmun stepped into the corral and trotted along with them toward the split rail fence.

A gunshot kicked up a spurt of dust at his feet. The horses, already jittery, whinnied with fear and began to scatter. One reared back suddenly and screamed. Another shot kicked into the dirt, but this bullet struck far from Hardmun, who had pulled himself onto the back of a gray gelding. He kicked at the horse's flanks and the animal darted forward. Hardmun caught a glimpse of the stringy-haired Glasser off to his right, standing on tiptoes on the bottom fence rail.

Trapped in the corral the horses rode in circles, their panic rising. Hardmun used this as cover, keeping low over the gray, out of Glasser's eyesight. Pulling on the pony's mane, he guided it toward the gunman, kicking the animal to greater speed. Glasser didn't recognize the horse's deliberate approach until it was too late. The animal skidded to a stop, lost its footing and crashed against the fence with its flank. Hardmun had braced himself and was ready when they struck. He flung himself away from the gelding just as Glasser fired a wild, frightened shot.

Hardmun slammed into the gunman and together they smashed to the ground. Glasser let out a pained grunt and began gasping for air as his bowler bounced away. Hardmun had rolled off the man and as he came to his knees spun around for his bearings. Frantically, Glasser clawed for his fallen revolver, his eyes wide with terror. Hardmun dove for the man, catching Glasser's wrist. He swung a heavy fist into the man's jaw and Glasser went limp.

A shot smacked against the nearest fence post. Hardmun swept up Glasser's fallen gun, swung it around to the back of the livery stable, and fired. He heard a ricochet and a yelp of surprise. Someone else peeked out through the barn door and Hardmun fired a shot at him. With one hand he tore at Glasser's gunbelt.

'Only makes it more interesting, Hardie,' Turk called out.

Hardmun fired another shot, taking a chunk out of the corner of the barn, then ran toward a house at the center of town. A woman screamed seeing him come and threw a pot at him. The thing clattered loudly as it struck a water trough.

'He's over here!' Tobler cried.

Wildly Tobler ran, firing recklessly. With his left hand he couldn't aim well enough to hit what he wanted. Hardmun ran from the house to a shed, found cover, and fired once. A bright red hole opened in Tobler's chest and the man nearly stumbled coming to a stop. Amazed, he looked down at his dirty shirtfront filling with blood. His left arm began to shake. After a moment he looked up, eyes vacant and misty, and crumbled to the ground.

'I don't need them to kill you, Hardie,' Turk called. Hardmun risked a glance around the corner of the shed but could not see the killer. 'Just you and me.'

'Then let's settle this, Turk. Just you and me. No guns.'

Turk laughed, the sound of it echoing in the street.

'I want you dead, Hardie. I don't care how I do it, but I want it done. So here you go.'

Hardmun heard a distant thump as something hit the ground. Cautiously he peered out from behind cover. Turk was standing in the open, arms held out to his side, his gunbelt on the ground. Thirty feet away was Turk's revolver glinting in the sun.

'Your turn, Hardie,' he said, grinning. Turk wore the look of a madman, but a clever madman. He had something planned.

Stepping into the open, Hardmun holstered his revolver then dropped the stolen gunbelt to the ground. With a sideways swipe of his foot he kicked it away.

Turk flexed his fists, still grinning. 'Good,' he said.

Hardmun took a step toward the outlaw when a shot cracked and a man cried out.

'Out in the open, you!' Ellen Vickers commanded. She had come suddenly out from behind the house with a rifle to her shoulder, holding it steadily at a broken down wagon left for scrap only a few short yards away from Hardmun. 'I said out!' she repeated.

His arms and gun raised, Bill Glasser sheepishly stepped into the open, a welt glowing red on his chin.

'You got women doing your fighting, Hardie? Never figured you for it.'

'Shut up, killer,' she spat. 'Link, pick up your gun.

We're getting these two to jail.'

Hardmun hesitated as he watched Turk's body tense.

'You didn't wait an hour.'

'No, I didn't.'

Crouching, his eyes always on Turk, Hardmun reached in the dust for his gun.

'It's a sad day, Hardie.'

Turk made no move for his gun. Instead, he laughed, and in doing so reached around his back. In an instant, a gun was in his hand and swinging up toward Ellen. Catching the movement out of the corner of her eye, Ellen pivoted, swinging her rifle toward Turk. At the same time, Glasser lowered his gun down toward Hardmun.

Throwing himself forward, Hardmun pinched off a shot that struck Turk in the leg. The big man spun and cursed, falling behind the corner of a building. Hardmun heard a buzz, then felt a tug at his arm at the same instant he heard the shot Tobler had fired. Rolling away, Hardmun snapped off three quick shots and instantly heard Glasser's muffled groan.

Grimacing with pain, Hardmun scooped up the gunbelt and ran to Ellen.

'Link, you're shot.'

The sleeve of his shirt was torn in two places and there were two bloody gashes on his right forearm. He almost laughed. His clothes were nearly in shreds anyway from the punishment he had endured for the past few days. And there were enough gashes and cuts on his body to make a new one hardly noticeable. Still, it hurt, and all he wanted to do was to lie down and go to sleep.

'Where'd Turk go?'

'Around the corner.'

Hardmun nodded. 'Stay here. And this time I mean it.'

Keeping low, he ran into the street. Turk was a few hundred feet away yanking at the long gun in his saddle boot. The horse provided cover but Hardmun didn't care any more. Turk had to be stopped. He fired two shots between the horse's legs and watched the outlaw dance awkwardly, heard him curse. The horse started to pull away, to run, and Turk, taking the only chance he had now, threw himself on to the animal's back and raced away.

Hardmun hurried to his own horse, leapt aboard, and chased off after Turk. The outlaw's cloud of dust was easy to follow out of town. They raced for several miles with Hardmun slowly closing the gap. As he neared he could see Turk had little control over his frightened mount. He was slipping in the saddle, too, frantically holding on with his weakened leg as he tried to clear his long gun from its scabbard.

Gun in hand, Hardmun raced up beside the outlaw. One shot, he thought. At this range that was all he would need. Instead, he swung the heavy gun down on top of Turk's head and watched with some pleasure as the man tumbled to the ground and landed awkwardly, smacking his head a glancing blow against a rock.

Hardmun reined to a quick stop and hopped from the saddle. Turk was still alive, trying to crawl to the rifle that had come loose at last and had fallen with him. The outlaw's leg was mangled and bleeding profusely. Hardmun could have shot him, then; wanting desperately to put a bullet in the man's head. Not trusting himself, he dropped his gun, then reached down for Turk, grabbing him by his shirtfront.

'I want to kill you, Turk.'

'Then do it,' the outlaw grinned. His face, a ghostly white and cut from the fall, hung slack and lifeless on the right side. 'I'm dead anyway. End it.'

Frustration welled up inside Hardmun before it burst out in a single punch that violently rocked Turk's head back. He found it odd that now that he had hit the man, his anger was spent. He let go of Turk's torn shirt and watched the man sink into the dust.

Ellen rode up and skidded to a stop.

'Is he dead?'

Hardmun shook his head. He was breathing heavily and every limb seemed made of lead. He stepped away from Turk to a low boulder and sat.

Ellen went to the outlaw, stood over him, hate coursing through her. Like Hardmun, she had purposely left her gun with her horse so as not to be tempted. She reached down and grabbed at the man's shirt. He was heavy but offered no resistance as she pulled him forward and slapped him. Turk replied with a lopsided grin.

'You can't prove nothing,' he said, slurring his words as if drunk. 'Your word against mine. As far as that town knows, I was helping the sheriff capture a desperate escaped murderer.'

Rage filled her and she slapped him again then let him drop. She was about to turn away in disgust when something glinting in the sun caught her eye. Beneath Turk's torn and bloody shirt there was a chain and a bit of gold around his neck. She pulled at it, snapping the chain easily. The gold was a wedding ring and on the ring, although she could not read it through the tears welling in her eyes, were engraved the words: *All my love forever, Peter.* Her sister had put this on the day she wed and never took it off.

'My sister's,' she told Hardmun, who had come up behind him.

'Is it enough proof?'

'It'll be enough. But Turk will—'

'He'll do nothing.' They looked down on Turk and saw that he had died. Ellen stared for long moments, numb from what she had brought about.

'So many dead,' she whispered. 'Link, I won't have any more killed over this. You have to ride away.'

'Ellen, I have to . . .' he started to say, but she put a hand up to his mouth, stopping his words.

'No. You didn't kill my sister. I know that now. I couldn't have stayed with you if I didn't believe that. If you stay, they'll just hang you. You think you deserve hanging, Link, but you don't. I don't believe you could ever have done something that was bad enough to hang you for it. You've been torturing yourself long enough. Let it go.'

'How can I?'

She smiled and lightly kissed him on the lips. 'Because I'm asking you to. Because I don't want you to die.'

'What about him?' A strange euphoria began working its way through him. He felt lighter than he had in years.

'I'll take him back to town. I'll tell them it's over.' She could see he was still hesitant. 'Go to California, Link. I'll find you.'

He pulled her close and kissed her, long and hard, and when they parted he said nothing. He lifted Turk's body onto his horse, throwing him crossways on the saddle, then boarded his own horse and rode away.

Alone, the old colonel surveyed the vast desert behind him. As with the posse that first hunted Link Hardmun and his gang, this new posse had also quit. They had captured some of the gang and that was enough for them. He was returning to town on a dead outlaw's horse, needing a fresh mount and supplies, and hoping to raise another posse.

The colonel was bitter but could not blame the men. They were dirt farmers and small-time ranchers, all of them cowed by the strong will of a vicious sheriff. They were needed at home. The colonel had no home other than his saddle, no responsibility other than his duty. So he remained.

Sheriff Capstin was someone else who rankled the colonel. This was someone who would have to be taken care of, the colonel decided. But not until after the fugitive was recaptured.

The colonel had just entered the town when he spotted a rider, perhaps two, coming in from the opposite end. They came slowly. As they neared, the colonel's sharp eye saw that one rider was slung lifelessly over his saddle. The other rider was a woman.

In time they met under the fierce heat of the sun.

'I have proof that this one killed my sister,' Ellen Vickers said, holding up the necklace and wedding ring.

The colonel studied on this, then nodded. That reminded him of the brooch he had taken from the dead outlaw and he dug through his pockets for a moment before finding it. He held it out for Ellen to see.

'That's my sister's,' she said quietly.

'I thought it might be.'

'She didn't have but two pieces of jewelry, and I gave her that one.'

'Found it on one of the gang. Someone who paid a call after you left me in the hills.' He wasn't bitter about that, though, or angry. In fact he smiled.

'I see you made it out just fine.'

'I did indeed, ma'am. That accounts for two of the

gang. What about the rest of them?' he asked her.

'Gone, every one of them. That gang is dead. And the sheriff and his men were part of it. They worked with this one. You'll find two of the deputies back of those buildings. The sheriff may be in his office, dead. This one here,' she said, tossing her head back at Turk's body, 'killed him. I guess they had a falling out.'

'And the other fellow? Hardmun?'

'Dead, too. Back in the desert. Turk got him.'

Nodding, the colonel said, 'You are quite some woman, Miss Vickers. Quite some woman. You'll show me where these men are?'

Ellen nodded. 'Let's get this one out of the sun, then I'll take you to the rest.'

The bodies were buried that night with little ceremony. The colonel announced that he was heading back East and would make his report, offering to accompany Ellen on her journey home. The following morning he asked after her but she was already gone.

And somewhere down the road the riders of a sorrel pony and blood red mare met up and traveled together to California.